THE ONES WHO FLEW THE NEST

Stories by Katie Hale, Louise Finnigan,
Jacqueline Ward and Helen Kennedy

Edited by Isabelle Kenyon

First published 12th of May 2023 by Fly on the Wall Press
Published in the UK by
Fly on the Wall Press
The Wentwood
72-76 Newton St
Manchester
M1 1EW

www.flyonthewallpress.co.uk
ISBN: 9781915789044
Copyright with individual authors © 2023

The right of the individual authors to be identified as the author
of this work has been asserted in accordance with the Copyright,
Designs and Patents Act 1988.

Typesetting and cover design by Isabelle Kenyon, imagery
Shutterstock.

Printed in the UK by Severn, Gloucester on responsibly sourced paper

This is a work of fiction, Neither the author nor the publisher
will be held liable or responsible for any actual or perceived loss
or damage to any person or entity, caused or alleged to have been
caused, directly or indirectly, by anything in this book.

A CIP Catalogue record for this book is available from the British
Library.

CONTENTS

YOU CAN LET YOURSELF BE SWEPT AWAY OR ELSE BECOME THE FLOOD

KATIE HALE

The first time they met, he told her one sweep of a wing could break a person's arm. She was pretty sure that was about swans, not geese – not to mention an urban myth – but she tucked her hair behind her ear and said, "Wow".

He flared his own wings like a magician's cape, and when he pushed out his long black neck and hissed, it was an acrid rush, like the valves in her old school science lab: a flare in need of a match.

He had planted himself halfway across Spenny Bridge, where the moonlight rang grey on painted metal and the river surged below them, dark and roiling. Up on Brampton Road, the streetlamps were distant orange beads. An unlit grassy slope before them. It was the sort of time her mum would have said was too late for cutting through the park alone, if her mum had known about it, which of course she wouldn't.

"Are you afraid?"

Her breath was sour against her scarf as she tongued the fug from her teeth. She thought she had forgotten how to be afraid. She tugged the old coat around her. "No."

"Good." His face shone thin and ghostly, his beak a dark stab from his eyes.

The second time, she hunched in the shadow of the bridge. She'd lugged the groceries across the park and stopped to rest, had told herself choosing this spot was an accident.

She left the milk to keep cold in the shallows, pushed her hair off her face and waited. When the Goose sidled up beside her, she dug her feet into the gritty silt at the edge of the river and said, "You never told me where you're from."

"From a barnacle." He puffed himself up at his own mythology. "From a hard crust in a rock pool – part land, part sea. See?" And he spread his wings to display the pale-edged strata running through them. "Each one is a tiny shoreline, caught between dark and light."

She wanted to say, "I read somewhere that barnacles don't have a heart." Instead, she asked, "Where do you live?"

"Far far away. You wouldn't know it."

"Tell me."

So he told her about summers on Spitsbergen – the endless light, the muted colours of the tundra. His stories smelled of cold oceans, of that sparkling blue freshness she'd always associated with the north. She had thought she'd find it in Carlisle, but not yet. He drew up his head as though pulled by string – the kind of posture exercise she'd been forced to undergo at ballet lessons as a child. "We migrate to the Solway Firth in winter."

She didn't ask how he'd ended up in the city centre, and he didn't admit to being lost.

"And you? Where have you migrated from?"

8

"Leicester."

"Ah." He shifted on scaly feet, close enough for her to feel the heat through his feathers, and when he swept a wing across her back, she let him.

After all, wasn't this why she'd come? Not just that afternoon, but to the city? To be away, to be free to walk across open ground with nobody accusing her? To give herself over to the desires of strangers? Besides – he opened his beak to rasp against her neck, pink tongue a flicker, a caught minnow – it was easy to make him want her. She let him nibble at the tip of her index finger, ran it along his beak, up the smooth arrow between his eyes. As she fetched the milk from the edge of the river where the cold water snatched at her hand, he tugged at a loose feather, told her she'd have to return.

"I'll think about it."

Then she sashayed her hips away from him till she reached the road.

The third time, she walked down through Rickerby Park on purpose. The grass was silver, plush, the dark footprints of pre-dawn dog walkers threaded through it like rubbed velvet. A river of mist smothered the line of the Eden, and the air tasted damp, pale. A mirage of droplets frizzed her hair from her scalp.

When he spotted her from the end of Spenny Bridge, he threw back his head and honked with raucous uninhibited glee. Across the river, a man and his terrier looked up in alarm.

"Follow me."

9

She wondered how he'd known she was coming. There was something triumphant in his arched neck, the way he stalked ahead of her, as if she were a racehorse he'd bet against, and won. She followed him away from the bridge, away from the path, into a scrub of bushes and stunted trees. The leaves that still clung to the twigs were dark and lank, ragged feathers, soaking her hair and clothes and skin. On the Goose's back, the droplets beaded like false jewels until he glittered. He pecked at her coat toggles and she undid them for him. "What is it you like about me?"

"Don't be needy."

"Tell me."

He rolled his head up the inside of her thigh, eyes closed, beak half open, soft, careful through the denim. "You smell like water. Like water that remembers it used to be ice."

So she unzipped her jeans and said, "Here."

When he entered her, it was with her face pinned to the mulching leaves, to the woodlice, to a crawl of centipedes, his beak tight in her hair. His wings beat fierce downdrafts against her shoulders, her neck, and she had to snatch the air from between them. She wondered if this was how it felt for people who claimed they'd had sex with angels: the body pushed to its limits, ecstasy in such an ordinary setting, the terrible overpowering of wings. The dew soaked through her knees and jumper, a baptism flooding her skin.

When he had finished, he folded himself neatly back together. She tugged up her muddy jeans and fastened her coat.

"Come back tomorrow."

"Maybe," she said, though she knew she would.

That night, as her flatmates' drunken laughter drifted up from the kitchen, she lay awake. Her textbooks hunkered in the corner of her desk, their glossy covers glinting in the half-light, as she waited for the dreams to come: disinfectant, her mum's rattled breath, dirty coffee from the machine at the end of the ward. They would come slowly, unstoppably, the way they had for the past two years – like polluted water seeping up between floorboards, sucking at the edges of the bed – and she lay in wait for them.

But tonight, she dreamed of wings, the nip and scrape of beak over her stomach, her breasts, the careful feathers fusing with her skin. She dreamed the smell of his body, till it took over her own – that wide northern tang, the smell of Arctic days that rolled into one another without break, that endless, dreamless light.

So he became a pattern, tessellating into her days. An addiction, though she couldn't tell which of them was the addict. On secluded sections of the riverbank, he entered her the way she knew he must enter other geese: erratically and with her face to the earth, so close she could hear the soil whispering its cold curses. She shut her eyes and let his wingbeats drown them out, and when she came, she came riotously – the way the winter did: sky a dark metal sheet that hurled itself at her and whipped dead leaves against her skin.

Over the weeks, she was sure the Goose grew slower. Sure he held himself inside her for longer, till she keened and her extremities grew numb. She was sure it was deliberate. Cold bled into her till all she could feel was him, commanding her body, baring her limits as he pushed her exultantly past them. There was an energy to it, an ecstasy, giving over to the beating span of his desires. She always returned home battered, soaked and shivering, her clothes a mess of mud and water. Her skin tingled in the kitchen heat.

In the last week of term, one of her flatmates dragged her into the city centre. His excuse was Christmas shopping. He was a Fine Art student – neatly painted nails, sculpted quiff that never missed a hair – and for the past month, he had been working in collage. He gathered titbits to him like a magpie: magazine clippings, event flyers, other people's lives. When she collapsed onto a bench in the shoe section of Debenhams, he eyed her over the top of his shopping list and said, "Ok, out with it."

"What?"

"The mystery man – woman – whoever you sneak off to."

People hurried past with Christmas mania in their eyes. She watched an old woman size up a shirt against her husband's back, the perfunctory touch turned tender as it passed between them.

"We've all been wondering."

"I go for walks a lot."

He smirked. "And come home with bed head. Sure."

"It's just a winter thing," she told him, scuffing at a mark on the fake marble floor. "It won't last."

But it was almost April before she felt the Goose grow restless. On their last day together, they sat on the grass in front of the castle, where she read to him from one of her course books and he laughed uproariously at the idea of debating stories that weren't even true. It was the first real warmth of the year. The red stone of the castle walls released the dusty scent it had kept locked inside all winter, to mix with the traffic fumes that thundered from the dual carriageway. Below, families and day-trippers emerged from the dark underpass, or trundled down the slope into its concrete mouth. She couldn't see the Cursing Stone from here, but she pictured them passing it, the polished granite gleaming like a gold tooth, its carved prayer like a seed caught in the gap.

In the other direction, a group of boys clambered the railings of the footbridge over the road and dared each other to make the jump to the high jagged edge of the old city walls. One by one, they teetered on the wrong side of safety, where cars and lorries buffeted below. Then, they leapt.

It took innocence, she thought, to do a thing like that. Innocence, or unrelenting guilt. Total faith the world would catch you, or reason not to care if it let you drop. She watched the boys break open smuggled cans of cider, all five now across the void, a kick of heels against the stone, already high on the rush of survival.

She asked, "How can you tell it's time to go?"

"Like breathing. Something my body tells me I need." The Goose shook out his wings. He'd been doing this a lot, lately, testing them, reminding her of his readiness to leave. He pecked a forget-me-not bruise on her breast. "Like I need you."

"I wish I could come with you." She'd told him this before, but today, imagining the great journey north and the space opening up beneath her, she wasn't sure she meant it. She wondered if there were any words that could make him stay.

"I could carry you. You could ride on my back."

It was her role, she felt, not to break these illusions, to remain complicit in his self-belief. So she stroked his head in her lap where he couldn't see her face and said, "Thanks for these months. It's been fun."

*

For weeks after he left, she drifted through the flat, hovered on the borders of conversations, picked at her food. Her flatmate cornered her by the open fridge to ask if she was pregnant. "Not to pry or anything," he said, spooning yoghurt into his avid mouth, "But are you?"

But rather than fullness, she felt emptied. She spent hours at her laptop, watching the cursor flicker in and out of existence, and when she did submit her assignments – late, half-referenced – they were what one of her tutors called 'a book club response'.

"Yes," she said. "What's wrong with book clubs?"

Her dreams returned, oozed into the bed so she would wake sweating, imagining the smell of her mum's perfume on the pillow, an itch like ants crawling over warm stones. She became restless. Her flatmate put it down to her mysterious break-up. He was taking a photography module on the side, and asked her to model for a series of sombre portraits in the drab graffitied corners of the city. He called it: *Love in Liminal Spaces: a photographic essay on the boundary between heartbreak and obsession, intersecting with the turbulent history of a border city.*

"Catchy," she said, and stared beyond the lens.

As the days lengthened, she found herself retracing her relationship with the Goose. When she mentioned this, the art student said there was a Nietzschean poetry in returning to the sites of past events, and maybe they should include those places in the shoot – a 'nostalgia sequence'. But she didn't feel nostalgic. She stood on the riverbank where she'd let him inside her and felt nothing.

Back in Leicester for the summer, she tried to scrub away the dullness, but it lingered under her skin like subcutaneous fat. To escape from the too-quiet house, she took on extra shifts at her old Saturday job in the chip shop, where grease clogged her pores and trapped the feeling deeper inside her. On late nights, she rolled her shoulders, sockets clicking, as if she could unfurl her arms and take off.

About once a week, her dad would corner her into stilted conversation. "You can talk to me, you know," he said once, staring into his sunken cappuccino. "Any time. Go for a drive, a walk around the park – whatever you like."

She tipped two extra sugars into the dregs of her latte, waited for the grains to sink through the froth. "We never did those things before."

Later, she sat on her old toybox beside her bedroom window, level with the sill, so if she blurred her eyes, she could imagine she was hovering above the patio, the street-stacked gardens laid out below her like piano keys.

"Barely said two words." Her dad, low and anxious, downstairs on the hall phone. Probably the only person she knew whose phone still had a cord, who kept himself tethered to something. "Ever since she left – before, even, not since –"

Silence. She picked a flake of paint from the window ledge, let it flutter into the dark behind the toybox.

"I'll come over." The click of the phone back into its cradle. A few moments later, her dad stood in her bedroom door, zip stuck halfway up his coat. He'd always had trouble with fastenings, always needed her mum to help. "Ok if I pop out?"

"Sure."

"I'll only be an hour or so."

She didn't reply. When she looked again, he'd gone. She waited till she heard the car edge off the drive and rev up to the main road before she moved, across the landing to her parents' bedroom. A glass of water ring-marked the bedside table – her dad was sleeping in here again. She opened her mum's wardrobe, wanting the familiar touch of her clothes, hanging limp, expectant, slightly damp – the way they'd been for the past two years – but it was empty. She tried the drawers, the ottoman, ratched through her dad's folded shirts and balled-up socks in search of something. Anything.

All she found was a suitcase under the bed – scant remnants of her mum's life, collected, shut away out of sight.

In the garden, she gulped the wet summer air. A robin watched from the fence, bold as its red breast, head cocked between her and the freshly weeded border. (When had her dad started gardening again?) She held out her hand, dipped her palm to suggest food. The robin hopped closer, only once, before a dog barked in the next garden and it took flight.

To take flight. A weird phrase. Taken from where, exactly? The fence, when she ran her finger across the top, was smooth, nothing taken from its sodden cross-pieces. From the air, maybe. Flight as an offering made by the sky, caught up by a pair of spread wings. She spread her arms, wondered what needed to be given in return.

In September, she moved back in with her old flatmates, in a different flat closer to the city centre. It squatted above a boarded-up pub between the castle and the supermarket. On the outside wall, a handmade wooden sign, level with her head, marked the height of the floods a decade before, and through her window – edges stuffed with old newspaper – the sad brown branch of the Caldew River crawled towards the Eden. Damp lingered in the plasterwork and spread black mould across the ceiling, so everything smelled of mud and rot and mushrooms. She bought reed infusers and lit scented candles. She strung cheap car air fresheners from the ceiling like bunting, but still the smell seeped through. At night, when drunken singing stippled the street and passing lorries rumbled her bedroom walls, she imagined the river rising through the stained beige carpet and up the walls, till it covered the bed and she was drowning.

She started the new term with a feeling of drifting. As she browsed the higgledy piggledy shelves of the second-hand bookshop, she tried to make herself invisible. It was a game she had played often, over the past two years – easy here, with the sprawling shop split and cornered by high shelves, where the rooms came round to meet each other like strangers on a railway platform. Books broke free of their alphabet: gathered in doorways, or peered like shy dogs from around the backs of armchairs. When she spoke, muttering the titles as she traced a finger along worn spines, the pages absorbed what little sound there was, till she imagined she could follow her voice into the age-spotted stories, let herself be translated into a fading line of text.

When classes started, the tutors' eyes skimmed over her, or else met hers for a fraction of a second too long, and she, like they, wondered why she had returned. She watched her classmates dissect works of literature like lab technicians scalpelling a dead frog. She had read somewhere, one insomniac night, about a Victorian experiment: an electric shock that caused the dead frog to spasm again with the false dance of the dead. But this kind of magic was beyond her. She carried her set texts to class like corpses, laid them at her tutors' feet like a pietà.

She took to wandering the city at strange hours. As summer surrendered itself to autumn, it was easier to find herself alone: the night-time fizz of possibility, every moment a page she could step through and lose herself. The streets hurried away from her; trees shrugged off their leaves at her approach. In the underpass below the dual carriageway, names of old border families tripped her from the floor and the Cursing Stone stood its concrete ground. The wind hissed through; it spat her out the other side like a denunciation.

It was this wandering that led her back to the Goose.

Huddled on a bench in the corner of the Chinese Gardens, she buried her face in her coat, knees pulled up to her chest. The gardens were not really Chinese. The scratched-up board by the gate described them as 'ornamental, in the Italianate style,' though to her the low hedges and seeding plants looked like any other flowerbed in the city. It was what she came here for: the lie of elsewhere.

Behind her, rush-hour traffic crawled across Eden Bridge and down to the roundabout, or up through Stanwix, out of the city towards the north. The gardens smelled of exhaust fumes and overhanging rain. On a bench slat, someone with a marker pen had scrawled SAVE ME.

The Goose appeared two terraces below, as though her being here had conjured him. He strutted between the trees and the ornamental hedge: landed gentry, she thought, a patriarch in a period drama, puff-chested, twitching his neck at the dimming riverbank. She played her invisibility game with the bench, till he strode away under the bridge.

She told herself not to think of him. For days, she shut herself in her damp and draughty bedroom and fought through impossible assignments, her head a chemical ache from the air fresheners. The old dreams still wailed and tumbled, but now they pinned her to the bed, or crumbled the walls of her sleep on powerful wings, and she always woke smothered in the duvet, its small and spiteful feathers scratching through.

So she put on make-up and a new jumper and returned to the Chinese Gardens.

The river raged, full and flailing after recent rainfall, and the bank was uneven where the current had bitten away the ground she used to stand on. When she spotted the Goose, unruffled at the water's edge, she was careful to let him think he'd seen her first.

"There you are."

Her arms prickled and she wanted to tell him how he shouldn't take her for granted, how at first she'd stayed away deliberately. But what would be the point? She held her palm to the stab of his beak and said, "You missed me." Then she led him to the unplanted space between the pergola and the boarded-up pavilion. *Love in Liminal Spaces*. She almost laughed.

For once, the Goose was gentle – bridged her skin with his beak, held her in the cradle of his wingspan. His feathers smelled of the wild, of the clear northern air trapped between their tines. He smelled of rock and spume and pine needles, of moss and ice and a weak sun. She breathed him in, the journey still cold and perilous on his wings, and when he collapsed his head onto her breast, she stroked the back of his long neck and hushed him the way she would hush a child.

Later, in the shower, she smelled the same wildness on her own skin, and when she scrubbed, the follicles on her arms tingled like something pushing through. She practised saying "I love you," and the words were a crisp wine she swilled around her tongue, chill, setting her teeth on edge.

In the weeks that followed, she began to hold her head higher, her arms lighter. She came home muddy, with leaves and sycamore keys in her hair, and spent more time in front of the mirror. Whenever he caught her on the stairs, the art student smirked and said thank god he'd got those photos before she went and fell in love again. But it wasn't love – at least, not hers. It was that this time, the Goose was not in the city by accident. Now, when he pinned her neck to the undergrowth, when his wings scrapped at her shoulders, instead of powerlessness she felt a beautiful complicity. She lay with her face to the dirt and pulled him inside her, revelled that he needed this more than she did.

Sometimes when he was finished, she asked about his migration, his summer in the north, and he would hiss like a quenched flame and change the subject. Each time, she thought she saw his eyes kindle panic.

She still went to classes. She took a module on myth and folk tale in contemporary fiction, where the tutor encouraged them to think laterally – "straying from the path," he called it, "leaving the breadcrumb trail behind to forage through the dark between the trees" – but as far as she could tell, they were just supposed to chop the forest down and count the rings. All of them, apparently, added up to sexual awakening. When she told this to the Goose, he laughed his brash honking laugh, then tugged her bottom lip between his beak.

Evenings when her flatmates were out, she brought him back to her room above the branch of the Caldew River. She bought end-of-day cut-price sandwiches from the supermarket next door, which they ate huddled over the pattern of cigarette burns in the carpet. She was surprised to discover he ate poultry – called chickens "pecky scratchy little shits" as he gobbled a stale club sandwich from its soggy wrapper. He ate eggs, too, and she found a perverse thrill in feeding him flaccid omelettes, stuccoed with black flakes from the pan.

Afterwards, she would bundle the duvet like a nest, would fall asleep curled around him, hugging his warmth to her stomach. She was never sure, on these festering nights with their headlights searching through the window, which of them was taking advantage of the other. Sometimes, when the Goose keened or whispered in sleep, she stroked his neck feathers to quiet him. Sometimes she lay awake to watch his sleep-fear spiral. Whenever her own dreams resurfaced, she pushed them down again, where they itched and irritated under her skin.

It was on one of these nights, as he twitched and whimpered beside her, that she noticed the change.

It was the tingling that woke her, pins and needles from her shoulders to the tips of her middle fingers. A prickle that intensified into a thousand small shooting pains, till she had to uncoil herself from the Goose and stumble to the bathroom. There, in the artificial light, she peeled off her shirt. Her arms had always been downy, dark hairs she had tried to shave off as a teenager, but now the hairs were bolder, thick with tines, and it stung when she brushed them in the wrong direction. When she plucked one with her flatmate's tweezers, a dark spot of blood beaded from the follicle, and when she dropped it, it spiralled lazily, drifted in the draught under the bathroom door.

In the morning, as she eased into a long-sleeved shirt, she felt the Goose's bright eyes on her. But she said nothing, and neither did he. The downy feathers rubbed against the cotton, persistent, the long dull note of a telephone left off the hook. She stuffed some books into a tote bag and left for class.

As the weeks passed, the feathers grew. They became sleek, dark, fringed with white like a salt-lick left behind by the sea. Instead of lifted, she felt cumbersome, a saturated towel, as the weight of her arms bloomed a heart-shaped ache at the centre of her back. They no longer tucked away into the narrow tubes of her sleeves. Each morning, she spent long procedural minutes fitting herself into oversized jumpers as the Goose nested among the blankets, his own wings tucked shyly away. Now, when they made love under the swaying air fresheners (was it love they were making?) it was slow and awkward, the Goose careful of her burgeoning pain, careful not to test her growing strength against him. Her arms measured themselves against the weight of her body and her muscles tightened. There was a smell, too – animal, wild, a rich addictive tang like skin two days since showering. Whenever she tried to wash it off, the water clustered on her feathers like droplets on a greasy tray.

She dropped out of her course around the end of term. Nothing formal. She just stopped going to class and ignored her assignments, though she carried on reading the novels. When the inevitable emails arrived from her tutors, then the department, then from Student Services, she let them sit in her inbox, each a locked door slowly rusting shut.

She took to wandering the city again. Sometimes, the Goose trailed in her wake – or else led the way, puff-chested, always turning back to check she was following. Sometimes she left him at the flat, hunkered in the bedroom with the light off. He rarely left without her, now, as though she were his shield against the world. She felt her body stretch and broaden in response.

Two days before Christmas, from a bench at the back of the castle, she called her dad to tell him she wouldn't be home. "I've got coursework – I need to stay and use the library."

"On Christmas Day?"

"I can work better on campus."

A silence on the other end of the line. She imagined him by the hall table in the lamplight, his ear fixed to the phone and the phone fixed to the wall, the rooms dark and empty around him. She watched a pigeon tug at a dropped poke of chips. His voice was quiet, "I miss her too, you know."

Another pigeon barrelled in, pulling itself up before it hit the pavement. What would it take to control the air like that? How much strength to lift herself from the ground?

"Are you still there?"

She watched as a pigeon thrashed a chip against the tarmac. "No. Sorry."

In the deep dark after midnight, when a fog had rolled in from the Solway and the streetlamps bled through it like crying souls, she took herself back to the castle. The dual carriageway was quiet as she climbed the stairs to the footbridge, another world from that broad spring day, when she had sat with the Goose to watch the boys leaping to their smuggled freedom on the old city walls.

She tugged off her jumper, released her splayed feathers. There was something eager about them tonight, how they tested themselves in the open cold. Not wings, exactly, but the potential for wings. She clambered over the railings, stood on the narrow ledge. She held on tight. From here, the jump seemed wider, the metal gate that barred the broken wall looked sharper, and the grass below rolled too quickly into hard pavement. She gripped the cold railing, shut her eyes. She let the fog drift between her feathers. Let herself listen to its gentle tug. She leapt.

She leapt, and she held back.

Even as she kicked off from the ledge, she knew it wasn't enough. Her head was too heavy with her own voice, her dad's *are you still there?* – and she scrabbled for the wall, then hurtled into the void.

She lay on the grass. Broken. Feathers skewed, her fingers bleeding. *Am I still here?* She stared up at the grubby underside of the bridge, the greasy fog-light beyond. A dull throbbing ached through her back, her shoulders, out along her wide and useless arms. *Yes*, she thought. *Unfortunately yes.*

Back at the flat, she let the Goose take her, wildly, fully, trying to find a way back to that overpowering winter, the feeling of disappearing under the strength of his wings. She lay with her face to the carpet – its cigarette burns, its smell of mud and receded river – and felt every cell in her body complaining its own existence.

Afterwards, she asked him what it meant to take flight.

"You seize it," he said, beak muffled against her belly, "from inside yourself."

She tugged a loosening feather from the back of his neck and said she wanted practicalities, not a motivational speech.

He hissed, "You take it with passion and great pride. A decisive action – the way you would take something that doesn't belong to you." And he nipped a bruise below her collar bone to show her.

From the top of the hill in Rickerby Park, they looked over the broad glinting threat of the Eden towards the city lights beyond. The grass, so smooth in daylight, was an ankle-trap of dips and shadows, and her arms tingled again. *Not arms. Wings.* She let the Goose push his head into the small of her back, let him tilt her forward till she began to run.

"Take it."

She spread her wings and felt the air spread beneath them. She pushed herself out into each feather, the exact point it tipped towards the sky, felt each one careful and deliberate as a weeded garden.

"Take it!"

I'm here, she thought, and then, *where am I putting my feet*, and then, *I'm already up.*

25

So that was that. The lights winked at her from below. The wind breathed into the gaps between her feathers, left half-whispered words nestled among the quills. She felt her shoulder muscles – what had been her shoulder muscles – work to hold her aloft as she flapped over the spidery black dash of Spenny Bridge, the churning river that might suck her down towards it, the scuffed and faded pitch markers of the school fields. *Yes*, she thought. *I can take this.*

She'd expected glamour, elation – at least a touch of awe. But it was just another way of moving through the world. A higher emptiness. Easier than she had thought it would be.

She circled back to the Goose.

Even from here, she could see the yearning, how he craned his neck to follow her, his desire transformed into something deeper. When she landed, clumsily, lumbering herself to the ground, he lowered his head, gazed up at her like an altarpiece. When she laid herself out for him on the frosted grass below the monument, he called her a wonder, and she believed him. She spread her vast wings till she imagined she could cover the whole city.

She started to realign herself to the Goose's aerial perspective, to see the ground as far away and optional. Now, whenever she was alone with him, she kept her wings uncovered, sometimes stretching so their tips brushed opposite walls of her tiny bedroom, or folding them across her back as she perched on the sill of the open window, ready to launch herself into flight.

Every night, they explored the city. She thought he might grumble, the way he did when she told him something he thought he ought to already know. But as she flew, and her wings strengthened, she thought she saw something in him rekindle, some new hunger for himself as well as for her, and she fanned it for both of them.

She took him to rooftops among aerials and satellite dishes, to the crenelated tower of the cathedral, the ugly grey grid on the roof of the Civic Centre. Wherever they put down, she pulled him inside her with the fierce new strength in her wings, till he gasped and honked and whispered, "Please."

Between the painted bays on the top of the multi-storey car park, she pushed his beak between her legs and let him taste her. His feathers fluttered against her calves as she held him there, his neck bowed and tense, spasming small breaths. There was salt in the air, driven in from the estuary by the onshore wind. She said, "When you go, I'm leaving with you." And into the soft wet of her, he gasped, "Thank you."

*

They left in the still blue moments just after dawn. By now the university had given up on her, officially, on headed paper. She sublet her room and called her dad to say she wouldn't be home for summer. She needed space to heal, she told him, because she knew he would accept that.

With nothing but a change of underwear and a calling, she lifted herself out of her old life, towards the north.

Beyond the city, the floodplains unrolled into cow-spotted marsh, which gave way to the curling grey tongue of the Solway Firth. Across it, Scotland stretched away from her in a tangle of peaks and clouds.

The Goose had timed it well. They arrived just as the flock billowed up from the mudflats: panic of wings, brash calls eager, disturbing the air so she had to steady herself against its new whorls and currents, as if it might pluck itself out from under her. She wondered briefly whether the other geese would allow it, a stranger in their midst, but as she slotted into the skein, they only glanced at her, curious and appreciative, as though she were a new child in a very small school. Beside her, the Goose puffed out his chest and they streamed northwards, beating a path for themselves across the sky.

*

The journey unspooled ahead of her, behind her, till its thread ran through her and it was all she could do to pull herself along it. The hills burst through their soft edges to become mountains, hard-faced and suspicious, with lochs imprisoned between them. She learned the tumble and plummet of a fellow bird, how the rifle crack always came after, over distance. She learned to fly on.

Whenever they stopped to eat and rest, in furrowed fields or at a lochan's sparkling edge, the Goose would press himself against her and whimper through his sleep. She kept her own dreams buried – easier here, pushing them under with every northward beat of her wings. She grew thin on a diet of roots and grasses. Hollow. So she filled the space inside herself with the barks and yips of the geese. Their stories travelled through her – stories of longing, of hard rock and great heights, stories of singularity within a group.

As they passed over the islands, the air grew colder and the sky laden with salt, and it became harder to hold herself aloft. They spoke less, though she found when she did call out, the skein would shift for her, make space where she needed it – a rippling pattern she let herself become a part of.

She could tell when they reached Spitsbergen from the taste: the air chill and newly lit, rising thermals laced with coal dust. Even before they landed, she could feel the difficulty in the earth – its unforgiving rock and freeze, a thing to be bargained with – and she remembered to be grateful to the air for keeping her up.

They put down on a stretch of rough cliff, far from any human civilisation: rocky stacks that plummeted away on every side, bare to the wind and occasional petulant blizzard.

"Stunning," she said, as they claimed their nook of stone.

Protection, the Goose told her, from the jaws of arctic foxes, and he shuddered and keened the way he sometimes did in sleep, his small fear lost among the raucous honks of the others.

Here, on the echoing rock, the flock's stories changed – became fraught with hope and hurry, frantic tales with unwritten endings, each one a small act of creation. She loved it, their future-spinning, their urge to vocalise everything. She gathered their stories avidly, the way she gathered the Goose inside her. After, he held her as though she were a precious jewel, something he could and needed to protect. Sometimes, he told her he loved her, and she said, "Thank you," or else, "I know."

She hardly slept, but it didn't make her tired. This far north, sleep had become a concentrated drug and the long days infused her with light. Her hair tangled with dust and grease, and a layer of oil glossed her weather-lined skin. Her stomach barrelled out till it matched his, and then surpassed it.

They made their nest in a dip of stone, high on the cliff. The Goose foraged on the grassy tundra, or in the shallows of the lake below. He delivered her dried grasses and moss for insulation, while she plucked downy feathers from the hinge of her wings. The nest sat empty, a waiting dish. For the first time since leaving Carlisle, she thought of her mum, the empty wardrobe, the suitcase tucked away under the bed like a forgotten story. She held the Goose inside her till it passed.

The eggs, when she squatted in the bowl of the nest to push them out of herself, were off-white and flawless, three marvels of her body's architecture. She had always known she could produce hardness, but the delicacy of the shells surprised her. She brooded over them, willed her warmth down into them while the Goose brought tokens – food, decorative sprigs of heather, a stone with a blue vein cracked through it. He refused to look at his incubating offspring. "An egg is an egg," he claimed. But sometimes, when he thought she was asleep, she caught him staring, and something flared behind his eyes, panicked as artificial fire. He's done this before, she thought. He's done this before and it ended badly.

And she settled more securely over the nest.

Around her, other eggs began to hatch: a plethora of small grey miracles that hurled themselves over the edge of the barren cliffs, tumbled on undeveloped wings to the rich tundra below. She didn't watch.

Her own goslings were born early one morning, before the Goose had left to forage. She had felt their impatient shifting, their worlds cracking open as the shells splintered, and they struggled into existence – three of them, wet and ragged, tiny cheeps that tugged somewhere behind her small intestine. As they pushed themselves out, she felt herself slipping away through the gap they left behind.

They flopped and tumbled in the downy nest, unfolded their formless wings among the fragments of shell. Their soft feathers dried in the sun, puffed out till they were more air than bird. She held a finger to each of them, let them nip at it. She whispered stories – of white-crested waves, the intricate map of coastline, how they would abandon the accidental city of their father to live wild on the mudflats of the Solway, fattening on moss and honeycomb worms as they waited out the winter – till her voice became the breeze they tried to lift themselves into, her words their only landmarks.

The Goose watched and said nothing.

"Aren't they beautiful?" She spread a wing as though their beauty was a small plan she had executed.

"They have to eat."

"So beautiful."

Their chirping grew louder. Hungry pleas – she felt them in her breasts, as though she had milk and could feed them. Could she? She rubbed her nipple between finger and thumb, till it was red and sore. The goslings' cries burst into starving wails.

"Come on," she whispered to her body, "Please."

"There's nothing for them up here." The Goose stared at the barren grey dust of the cliff, spoke sharply on an in-breath. "They need to take the leap."

"No." She kneaded again at her breasts, bullied them with her fingers and fists. "No."

The first gosling threw itself from the cliff.

Her body was a cry caught in the throat as she threw herself after it – its downy wings fighting to keep it upright – the rock face – her gosling's tumbled weight. She saw it bounce on a moss patch on the tundra, saw it lift its head, ruffle its wings – saw the fox slink from the foot of the cliff, audaciously sleek, rippling in the sun. She saw it snatch her gosling in its maw and steal back into the shadows.

"No," she said to the scree and the dust. "No, I take it back."

But the ground up here was a shoulder turned away from her, and when the second gosling plunged closer to the cliff face, she heard it crack against the rock, go still.

She threw back her head and screamed. The Goose, the flock, the entire Arctic shrank from her rage. She launched herself at the clifftop, snatched her last gosling from the edge. He felt solid in her grip, a fragile lie, and she understood now where flight was taken from. She took it from the clifftop, from the jagged rocks and from the waiting jaws of predators. She took it from her two dead goslings and gave it to her one remaining child. She stole her flight, and for the first time, the air fought her for it back. She carried her weight unevenly. Her wings dragged on the side she held her gosling, threatened to spiral them both to the ground. She gritted her teeth – such a human expression for perseverance – and told the air no.

They landed clumsily, in the tussock grass at the edge of the lake, lay recovering in a tumble of feathers and fear.

"When I was sixteen, I started to have this dream." She whispered it into his soft feathers, into his smell of dust and dew and cold light, "About my mum, about how she wouldn't survive the treatment. It was a nightmare, except it wasn't, I didn't feel afraid. But then when it happened, it was like it was my fault. I dreamed she wouldn't make it, so she didn't."

She led him out onto the safety of the water, let him feed from the grasses at the fringe. Already a sharp black arrow pulled his eyes down towards his beak, his whole body pointed towards the future.

"And I'm done now," she told her gosling. "I'm done paying for it."

All summer, she worked to raise him on the tundra, guarded him from foxes, from the hooked ferocity of the gulls.

Sometimes, the Goose tried to help. More often, she saw him eyeing the female geese, sidling up to them with his chest out and neck extended, always with one backwards eye on her. She let him. She washed out her hair in the meltwater, ran her fingers through it till it relinquished its tangled nest. When she sat, it was with one leg crossed under her, the other stretched out in front, wiggling her plump toes solely because she could. Once, he sidled up to her, pecking for the nape of her neck, a desperate hiss lodged at the back of his throat. She pushed him away.

The days turned colder. Brief darknesses dipped the sun below the horizon and the first light flurries of snow left her huddled in the grass. As the flowers and heathers trimmed themselves back for winter, the gosling grew leaner. His neck lengthened and his wings unfurled like flags, and she would catch him spreading them, measuring their reach. His tufty down moulted, to be replaced by long grey feathers that grew in fits and patches, leaving bald mammalian skin in their gaps. He never spoke, and she never tried to make him — though during the expanding nights, she sometimes heard the Goose, failing to coax him into small, slow words. By the time the flock gathered for the migration home, the Goose had given up.

The journey south was colder, more desperate than the journey north. Her gosling shivered alongside her as they fled — fled the dark, the cold, the winter's ice-white creep across the Arctic — and she urged him onwards, their own isolated struggle in the endless weeks of the skein. When gunshots rang up from below, she barely faltered, drove on as another of them tumbled, willing her gosling in her head when she had run out of energy to speak.

When they finally approached the Solway, the noise from the flock grew like a tidal wave. They pushed it ahead of themselves, a last exhausted sweat towards the mudflats and their winter rest. A jubilation.

She watched them drop down over the peat bogs, the sparkling silver firth. Her gosling made to follow them, but she pushed on, leading him in her slipstream. She had had it with grasses and mealworms and stink. She wanted walls. She wanted chocolate and tinned soup and watery sliced ham in a flat plastic packet. She wanted indoor plumbing and a bed. She urged him on, to where the orange lights of the city sprawled away to the south.

The flat above the river was empty, the windows boarded. Outside, the pitiful branch of the Caldew had risen with a recent storm, to seep its brown ooze into the brickwork of the retaining wall. A TO LET notice hung precariously above the door. Inside, the flat smelled fungal, condemned.

She gathered whatever had been left – warped furniture, damp-spotted books, curtains she tore from the plastic rails – to make a nest on the floor of her old bedroom. There was running water, enough chipped and rusting kitchenware to make do. She lifted an end-of-summer camping stove from a display outside the supermarket, changes of clothes from bags left in the doorway of a charity shop, and started to fit herself back into the city. It was easier than she expected. Nobody to hold her accountable. The bank, once she had answered a few security questions, were quite happy to send a new card to her old address. She covered her wings with a wide-sleeved jumper and, in the driving autumn storms, nobody looked at her too closely.

Whenever she left the flat, the gosling tried to follow, and she had to fling herself out onto the pavement and slam the door behind her. As she turned the key, she would hear the scuffle of his wings at the letterbox.

"They wouldn't recognise you," she told him one evening, as he tugged his beak along the gap in the window boards. She stirred baked beans over the camping stove, watched for the slow steam. "It's not safe."

He launched himself at the pan to scoop an orange beakful.

"Hey!"

The gosling turned back to the window cracks, wing sweeping dismissal across her face.

"It's better this way." She made her voice soft to not abrade his featherless skin. "Promise."

*

When the Goose arrived in late November, it was as he always did, unannounced and with his beak seeking the back of her neck. She returned from the supermarket – fought her way in past the gosling's flapping at the door – and found him in the kitchen, wings tucked behind his back like a Victorian headmaster.

She dropped the bags and the gosling tore the packaging from a loaf of bread. "What do you want?"

"To talk." His eyes glinted at her covered wings, at the space between her legs.

"So talk."

He watched as the gosling hauled slice after slice out onto the stained linoleum. "Not here."

"Fine."

Leaving the gosling distracted by the groceries, he followed her back downstairs and out into the drizzle. The headlights carving up the dual carriageway lit everything silver, so for a moment, even the Goose looked soft and noble. She didn't offer to help as she waited for him to tug the front door to. "Well?"

"Walk with me."

He led her down the side road, out past the trampoline park. Past the industrial estate, its flood-lit forecourts, where the biscuit factory smell of butter and ginger drifted between the chain-link fences, settled like warm fog in the deserted streets. She knew where he was taking her, but she asked him anyway.

"You'll see."

By the time they reached the footpath by the side of the river, the city noise had dropped away. There was only the distant beep of a reversing lorry, the thrum of cables overhead, and the constant churn of the water on its way to the firth. The footpath was deserted. She took off her jumper and her wings clicked and whispered as she stretched them free. The Goose spread his own wings in reply.

He wanted her — she could tell from the dip and rise of his neck, the way he fixated on her breasts. She lifted her vest top over her head and saw him go still, saw the veneration blazing in his eyes. Just like any other man, she thought. "What did you want to talk about?"

"Don't leave me again." His plea was a whisper, and the rumouring river carried it away.

She let him look for a heartbeat longer, then got dressed again. As she led him back along the river path, past warehouses and corrugated depots, she told him about the gosling. How he liked the seeded bread, and would peck her bloody if she only brought home white. How he invented games with empty tin cans. How he would shunt them across the bare floors so they clattered and clamoured at the skirting.

"He doesn't belong here."

She teetered on the edge of the curb. "Where?"

"In the city. He's not like us."

"He's mine."

"Ours."

She stuck out her chin, as though she could draw her head further from her body, the way he did. "He belongs with me."

"I'm sorry."

The front door swung on its hinges, and the takeaway menus from the stairwell whirled across the dual carriageway. She pushed through, up the stairs and into the flat, calling, calling for her gosling. Outside, she darted down side streets, leaned over the railings to stare into the muddy branch of the Caldew, its growing fury. Her eyes raked the stream of retreating brake lights crawling towards the roundabout. Twice, she scoured up towards the hospital, down by the old cotton mill, looped the castle to stare into the receding park for her gosling's gangly lope, his half-feathered silhouette above a streetlamp.

When she slogged, defeated, back to the flat, she found the Goose, still and silent in the middle of the kitchen.

She said, "Why are you here?"

"I missed you."

"And our son?"

He drew a foot across the floorboards, tracking a webbed road through the dust.

"You missed the city, not me."

He bowed his head as though waiting for absolution. "I had to let him out. It's for the best."

Her cry was a screech, a squall, a fury more goose than human.

He said, "But we can start over…"

She let her silence expand till it filled the room. It squeezed into the broken cupboards, nudged against the damp and mouldering walls, then out through the cracks in the boarded windows. It spread over the dual carriageway, the supermarket carpark, over the cobbled streets of the historic quarter and the dark unlit grounds of the cathedral – towards the industrial estate to the north and the racecourse to the south, over pubs and offices and estates and cul-de-sacs, out towards the motorway, the estuary, the Solway Firth. She let her silence spread till it pushed against the hovering clouds and the clouds hurled it back to her as rain.

As the first drops lashed against the window-boards, she turned her back on him and went to bed. She lay and listened to his betrayal battering itself on the roof. A torrent was welling up inside her, and she fought to keep it down. Hours later, when he joined her on the mattress, she felt him fold his wing across her like a prison door sliding shut, and she couldn't tell whether she was inside or outside the cell.

All that week, the Goose shuffled around the flat, dust eddying in his wake, as though he could blend into the slanting shadows, convince himself back into her life. She spent most of her time outside.

Christmas shopping season had started, and families in dark coats dashed from shop to shop through the grey beat of the rain. Some days, sodden and shivering, she wandered the wide brick laneways of the shopping centre, where giant red and gold baubles hung clustered from the glass roof. They looked too heavy for it, as if a word spoken at the wrong pitch might snap the thin wires, and they would drop and crush her.

She stood underneath them and hummed experimentally.

From a stand near the bus station, she bought instant coffees in polystyrene cups, which she cradled on the steps of the Market Cross, letting the wet plaster her hair, letting it soak up through the seat of her jeans. She jumped at the close whirring of pigeons, the wingbeat of a promotional banner in the wind – and once she stared for a whole minute at the back of a loping teenage boy.

She started to find feathers around the flat – sleek grey scatterings she threw away without comment, while the Goose pretended not to notice. On the few occasions he went out, he returned with pilfered newspapers and flyers for tourist attractions, the ink run, coming apart in the rain. He hid them in the gaps behind the sink and at the side of the cooker, where she could happen on them accidentally. She never looked at them.

Now, whenever she left, she paused in the stairwell to listen to him pacing, endlessly pacing the mildewed rooms, his webbed feet heavy and irregular against the hammering of rain at the door. Sometimes, she thought she could hear a soft silted whisper from under the floorboards, pictured the river, seeping through the brickwork, beginning to gather in the space below.

She used the library computers to message her old flatmate. *Long time no see – fancy a coffee?*

Alert and gossip-hungry as always, he replied within minutes. He was free Saturday – they should catch up.

They met in the bookshop's new café. So soon before Christmas, the place was crowded with chattering shoppers, thick coats dumped over the backs of chairs and umbrellas dripping by the door. With so much breath and gossip, the little windows had steamed up, so the figures hurrying down Long Lane were dim and half-conjured. Inside, everything smelled of damp wool and coffee and fresh baking, a rich golden smell that cushioned the ache in her chest.

"Only been open a couple of weeks," the flatmate informed her, with the air of someone who catalogued the city's news, ready to unroll it like sequinned ribbon. "The cheese scones are to die for." Then he told her about his open studio exhibition, and the London gallery who were interested in a couple of his pieces.

She spooned sugar into her latte and nodded along. Her shoulders pulled from her spine like tow ropes and she imagined letting go, unfurling her wings here in the crowded café, crashing sugar bowls and teacups against the walls. The image felt so absurd that she wanted to sob. She turned it into what she hoped was a cry of joy about the exhibition.

"Yes, isn't it?" the flatmate said, though she was sure she hadn't actually said anything. "And what about you?"

"So so."

He eyeballed her over the top of his cappuccino. "You know, I always thought – you know when we took those photos? Like there was something hidden, something shut up inside you."

Dust had gathered on the needle of the record player beside them, so the carols crackled and skipped. She took a gulp of coffee that burned her mouth.

"Are you happy?"

"Is anyone?"

He placed his cup back on his saucer. "Happiness is the feeling that power increases."

"What?"

"Nietzsche."

She rolled her shoulders to try to loosen the ache and felt it shift down into her lower back. "And what the hell does that mean?"

"It's like, happiness is based on feeling as if we have agency in the world. You know, power. Control." He repositioned his cup to align the handle with the folded slant of his napkin. "But it's bullshit."

"Right. I thought you loved Nietzsche?"

"I did, once." He placed a hand on hers, and she jolted at the human touch.

By the time they left the café, the city was grey with rain. It bounced off the tarmac like spits of oil from a hotplate and cars scattered their headlights across the pavements. She said goodbye to her flatmate, who pulled her into a quick hug. She thought she saw him startle at the bulk of wings under her jumper, but before she could say anything, he was gone, lost among the hooded figures dashing from doorway to doorway.

She made her slow way back towards the flat. She let the rain slick her hair, let it run down her face and slip cold hands under her coat collar. In the brief shelter of the underpass, she listened to the thunderous echo of so much water, the roar of traffic overhead. The museum's underground gallery looked dark and blurred through the thick glass panels in the wall, as though it was already underwater.

At the tunnel mouth, she ran a hand across the polished granite of the Cursing Stone, traced the carvings of its ancient prayer. She had done this ever since she moved to Carlisle, whenever she passed – a superstition, a wish. A plea for forgiveness. But today she stood without thinking. The stone was cold to touch and the words chiselled into it were nothing but letters. She walked back out into the deluge.

The pain in her back was nagging now, louder as she grew closer to the flat.

She pictured the Goose puffed up in the kitchen, his brochures and tabloids clogging the edges of the room as he strewed the floor with his feathers. She was sure, now, that he plucked them out deliberately. She tried to remember the last time she had seen him fly.

She turned and staggered away from the flat, dodging the blared horns across the dual carriageway, up the narrow letting of Milbourne Street, where the pavement was edged with wild scrub and the bank fell away into the Caldew. She needed to be next to the water, its potential for fury, its relentless vocal surge.

In the shadows of bushes and trees, she shed her coat and her jumper so the rain could streak across her wings. She slipped in the mud and caught herself on a branch, tearing her palm. She stripped off her vest top and her jeans and let the wind rip at her, felt the scourge of twigs and thorns, till she was no longer human, no longer goose, till the storm was inside and out, and she couldn't tell if she was screaming or drawing breath. The Caldew had become a riotous braying thing on its charge to join the Eden. The dark water churned and frothed. It threw out licks of current to try and snare her, as she squatted at the edge of its terror, clung to a flimsy branch for support.

She lost track of how long she waited there. She thought of the Goose with his wings folded smugly behind his back. She thought of her gosling, pushing gleefully through the swirling takeaway menus to grasp his freedom from the polluted city air. She thought of her mum, as upstream, the rivers strained at their banks – then burst. Water swept through the city, spread its slick ooze through the estates, gurgled up sewage from below. Fuel stations spilled petrol into the murk. Faraway sirens cut through the gale, then went quiet – and still the rain fell.

All night she let it soak her, let it swirl up around her, then drop back, only to swirl up again – till a grim grey glow lit the clouds to the east, and distant noises broke through as the city woke to its destruction. She spread her wings and launched herself above it.

All across the city, the Eden had reclaimed its ancient flood plains. Families clustered at upstairs windows, their kitchens and living rooms given over to grief. It took root in swollen skirting and saturated the furniture. It embedded itself in the walls of a thousand homes. She pictured the Goose, caught in the abandoned coffin of the flat and flapping, powerless, scattering pieces of himself as the water oozed up between the floorboards.

How could anyone recover from such chaos? The swell had drowned street after street, had bumped the cars up against each other, brown and broken like a stack of excavated bones. Sickly yellow froth bubbled from the drains and river-churn, snagged on the underside of Spenny Bridge. In the low-hanging branches of trees on Warwick Road, plastic litter caught and pulled with the current, drifted out over submerged gardens. It made her think of her dad, stooped over the border at the edge of the lawn in Leicester. His care in nurturing each small flower towards the light. She wondered whether any phones in the city were still working, whether she could still call the tethered landline on the table in the dim-lit hall.

As the last of the dark lifted, she watched the murky water skeining in the wake of rescue boats. As the army lifted people from windows or waded them through the shallows, the first skips arrived, and families began to assess the damage, to anticipate what would be needed to rebuild.

In refuge centres on the fringes of the city, coats and blankets were being gathered and shared. Cups of tea passed from hand to hand, and with them, voices. Grieving, complaining, urging each other on. They threaded together, rose from the deluge to where she hovered above it on her strong wings. As she listened, each word became a sadness, then a tribute, then a small, ascending warmth.

IVY WIFE

LOUISE FINNIGAN

The garden wall has been built so high that now the sky looks smaller.

"See how we're not overlooked anymore," Rob says.

She can only nod.

"It's the ultimate privacy feature," he adds – hoping, perhaps, for her approval.

She nods again, tries a smile.

She has heard it being constructed of course, over the previous weeks. The voices of workmen, the drone of machinery. But still – waking up to it after her whole week in bed, coming out to where she can actually see it – it's a shock. The whiteness of the rendering makes it look as if the walls have no corners, no edges. Just their house, their land and then nothing.

Now, she sees their garden as if for the first time. The wall's neatness makes it seem suddenly so shabby and wild; the grass is long and leaf-strewn, and the weeds seem to have shot up without her noticing. But then, she's been too busy to notice anything beyond her missed deadlines, her failing body, her frantic journeys from work to clinic, from clinic to work.

Now, she notices how the ivy is creeping over the roses and wrapping itself around the trees. It is beautiful and at the same time threatening. Its broad leaves shine and quiver in the sunlight, as if somehow animate, excited.

She says, "There's quite a lot of work to be done out here."

"But you're going to have so much more time for this kind of thing now, aren't you?" Rob spreads his hands to demonstrate how everything is working perfectly, how it all falls so neatly into place.

"Yes," she says, "I suppose I will."

She turns away from him, goes back inside and pours herself a glass of water. "Louder," she tells the house, and the sound of hearthwife rises against the running tap. There is so much happiness, it reminds her, in remembering what it is like to simply give. The modern world teaches us to take-take-take, and we fall into this trap of accumulating privileges we're too busy to even enjoy! I understand only too well how— She drinks deeply, then remembers herself and pours a glass for Rob. Takes it back out to the decking where he is scrolling through messages, stretching his muscles in the sun.

They stand next to one another. The new walls mean there is no longer a view of next door or their garden. No more having to look away as a pram is pushed up and down the gravel, or as a cartwheel competition takes place on the grass, or as water is sprayed in a sparkling mist over a small, tumbling body.

*

Fertility notifications are synched across their devices, and this means they don't have to discuss it anymore. It is better not to discuss it: her brokenness, his perseverance in the face of all evidence. It has been four days since she got out of bed into her new jobless life, and the date is flashing up green on her calendar. When his car pulls into the drive and he finds her in the garden, they do not talk.

He is right about there being absolute privacy. Down by her feet, a gardening glove is left splayed and empty. Beside them is a row of terracotta pots, then the geraniums in their plastic trays. When he finishes, she will kiss him and mutter something hopeful in his ear and then, she supposes, she will just carry on with the garden. It is good to feel each small task properly completed. Today the geraniums, tomorrow the ivy. It is manageable. Even the pain of their almost-certainly-fruitless sex is manageable, in this new, smaller world.

He is done. He steps back, and she straightens her dress. From inside the house, hearthwife has cut out mid-word, so she knows a call from Rob's work is coming. "I'm already on it," he tells someone as he zips himself up with his free hand. "I'm booking the flight now." She bends to pick up the dropped glove and reminds herself of the pleasure that is to be found in giving.

This is what they agreed upon that week, in the darkness of the bedroom, after the row with Sally. She knows it is the right choice. A quieter life. A gentler way to be in the world. Now, as hearthwife often tells her, there will be less stress.

More chance for nature to take its course. And it's possible the sentiment might be right, although out of all the kind and reassuring phrases about fertility, she hates this one the most.

She has almost, but not quite, given up imagining it: the tiny limbs somersaulting within the walls of her own skin.

Rob has finished on the phone and is going back into the house, calling over his shoulder about the ivy. She admires the abundance of it; how it crashes and collects around the tree roots in green, glossy pools, then comes to a halt at the end of the grass where the wall glares back.

"That stuff needs ripping out," he is saying from the decking – semi-thoughtful, about to roll out the suitcase for another trip – "before it starts to get out of control."

*

This time he will be gone for over a week, and she creates a mental checklist of tasks so she can show she has achieved something by the time he comes home. It is another fiercely hot day and she reminds herself how lucky she is to have the air-conditioning of their home, the shade of their walls. She spends most of the day in the garden – absorbing the light and shadow, breathing in the thick, green air. Finally, she breaks into the orderliness of his shed to search for the secateurs and carries them, gleaming, across the lawn. *hearthwife* is turned up as loud as it will go and the voice rattles the windows, shivers the leaves.

There's a particular type of madness that comes from trying to be all things to all people. I used to be sucked into all that kind of stuff myself and I still remember how frantic I was, how much failure I felt each day. I was trying to meet every target and demand instead of focusing on what was right there in front of me: my husband, my home, my life. These are not unimportant things, to be 'got to' later. These are not things to be neglected.

She knows the trees will be compromised if the ivy grows any further. There is a poem about it she half remembers from school. The ivy creeps higher and higher to rival the tree, overshadowing him, pulling at his bark with her waxy claws. And the man laughs – or is the woman who laughs? – when everything comes crashing down at the end. It had always unsettled her, even then. There can be no winners – that's what the poem seems to suggest. But she is forgetting herself again. She should be taking care of the task in front of her. She crunches into the woody stem with the secateurs and winces at the slash of light green flesh.

By the end of the day, she has crammed the huge waste-tub with ivy until it is full to the brim. Some of it trails from under the lid like the green, tumbling hair of a giantess. She notices, as she rolls it all out to the front of the house, that next door must have had a party. Children holding balloons are being clicked into safety harnesses and driven away. All day they must have been crashing and laughing through the garden. They were less than a hundred feet from her, and she did not know it.

Maybe it's the walls doing their job and keeping her apart from her neighbours or maybe, she thinks, it's because she herself is changing. Becoming resigned to it all. Allowing herself, finally, to move on. She looks down and sees how the blood from the ivy has run into the lines of her palms.

*

Rob comes home, and she concentrates hard on the joy of seeing him as she lights the candles and makes the dinner.

"You know your hands are dirty," he tells her as she puts the knife and fork down on the table in front of him.

"From the garden," she says. "I'll go and wash them."

His eyes follow her to the sink where the water splashes over the flush of her skin. "I didn't mean to criticise," he says. "You're looking well. I think maybe something's different."

She turns off the tap and moves back towards him. "I do feel different."

"Different as in... hopeful?" He leans towards her in the candlelight.

"No. Not really that. But different in a good way. More rooted in my body, I suppose."

"It just proves you've made the right decision. I'm proud of you." He starts to eat. Chewing his asparagus he says, "It might be a good time to make that call now. You know, with Sally. Finalise it."

She watches his steak knife sawing into the meat, the sliver of green between his teeth.

"We don't need the money," he says. "And look at you! You're already stronger than you were."

She looks down at her hand again, flexes her fingers. Behind the glass, the walled garden rustles in the dark.

*

"Call Sally," she tells the house. Rob's car has just left for the airport again and hearthwife is paused, as if holding its breath.

Are you sure you want to call Sally, the house asks.

"Yes. Go ahead."

There is silence for a moment. Then the throb of each dialling note as she waits.

"I take it you're not coming back." The voice on the other side sounds flat, betrayed. Sally will have been drowning in it all, without her.

"It's just to confirm my decision," she says.

"Your decision?"

"Yes."

She hears Sally's chair being drawn up to the big, shared desk in the centre of the office. The place where they used to arrange their quinoa and kale into virtuous platefuls before abandoning it for stashes of chocolate hidden in the recesses of old filing cabinets. Where they would play catchphrase bingo while taking conference calls – Sally hitching up her pencil skirt and running around in silent circles, punching the air because someone said, "Let's not get ahead of ourselves." Oh, how they had got ahead of themselves. Nominated twice for the Trailblazer Awards. Calculating strategies to take down their older, more established rivals. Messaging Rob to order food in because she'd be working late. Sally pumping the milk out of herself to send home to the nanny she'd hired. The sound of protest on the street below. Another strike. Another march. The warnings of the coming storms. The sight of the breastmilk right there on the desk between them, going cold.

"I won't be coming back," she says, fixing her eyes on the

square of a kitchen tile.

"Why though?"

"You know why."

"I want to hear it from you."

"Because some women are meant to stay at home. Instead of trying to be everything. I can't be everything..." She imagines Sally's face. The pity. The carefully concealed impatience. Pathetic – that's what Sally must think. It had all come so easily for her.

She tries a different tack. "Since I left, I've been..." She stretches for it, knows it is wrong but says it anyway. "Calmer."

"But I know you," Sally says. Her voice is soft, but it doesn't mean the words aren't going to hurt. "I know you so well. And you don't sound calm. You sound worse than the day you left. You just sound kind of ... empty."

She hears the word and imagines the little, wanted body inside her own. The phantom flip and flutter. She cannot stand it. In the creases of her knuckles, she sees the green. Paler as she opens her fist, brighter as she clenches it again.

"Hang up," she tells the house.

And it does.

*

The next day the rains come, heavy and dark. So loud against the windows that the sound of hearthwife is almost lost and she has to turn it up and force herself to concentrate.

Only a few years ago these words would have been met with outrage. I was called a bigot. I was called a traitor. And all because I dared to say the words they already knew. She watches water stream down the glass as she listens. Tries to calm the restless anger in her blood. *Women were happier before. Before the fantasy of equality. Before the contradiction of feminism that wrapped itself around our oldest traditions, strangled the life out of all we held dear. Our boys, our men, were being suffocated and belittled. Pushed to the very brink!* There is an itch under her skin that seems to rise as the day goes on. By nightfall, it almost burns. *Our way is not easy*, she is told as she scratches at her arm, watching herself in the dark of the window. *Our way means women making sacrifices. Women throughout history have always made sacrifices. But you may find that what you give up is nothing compared to what you gain.*

Then the episode is over. The house is silent. She wonders, *what have I gained?*

Outside, there is only the answering fury of rain.

*

"Three of our neighbours are getting it done," Rob tells her, walking across the grass. The water has finally retreated, and everything is steaming in the heat.

"Getting what done?"

"Walls just like ours. Same company and everything. We must be trending."

"Trending?"

"And it's not just the walls either. Jon from across the road – his wife has come back to the home as well. She's never been happier!"

But it is hard to understand him. His words, any words, have started to feel distant, as if on the other side of a membrane. Increasingly, she hungers for quiet – for the softness of birdsong and air. She leans forward on her knees and scrabbles a hand into the soil, wondering if he will go away again soon, leave her to her thoughts.

Behind her, he pulls at a leaf, and she hears it snap as he speaks. "I thought you'd cut the ivy."

"Yes. I did."

"There's still loads of the stuff. Swarms of it."

"It grows back faster than you'd think," she says, turning and looking past his head. A creature with papery wings flits between them. A small spider glides down a thread. Tiny tendrils of moss wander over their world of bark. And the ivy, barely diminished, climbs.

*

On the nights he spends at home, he does not touch her. He is too frightened in case he dislodges what he hopes is growing inside her. She knows he is wrong, but it doesn't hurt like it used to. Not in that long, hollow way that came with each late bleed. "It's not your fault," Rob would say, as he cradled her. Then, on other days, "You're working too hard," as he packed his suitcase again and booked his ticket to wherever he was going. Lisbon, Sydney, Dubai.

Now, she watches him sleep until he blurs into vagueness.

She feels her limbs, strong and lithe under the sheets, and holds the pads of her fingers to her face, imagining tiny shoots bursting from the tips. Roots of lightning made flesh. She listens to *hearthwife* but the sound only scratches against her in the dark. "Stop," she says suddenly, and her voice cracks like a whip.

Are you sure you want to stop mid-episode, the house asks.

"Yes. Please stop."

Would you like recommendations for podcasts similar to hearthwife?

"No. No I wouldn't."

Next to her, Rob doesn't stir.

"Delete it," she says and joy shivers through her.

*

He has gone again but she forgets where. She spends her days in white, trembling sunlight, her nights in humming wakefulness. She wanders over slices of moonlit floor, reaching out into the corners of each room as if trying to pluck something she cannot articulate from the narrowed air. *No*, she thinks. *This isn't enough. This isn't enough, at all.* She trails past items that seem suddenly made for a doll's house: a teacup, a scented candle, a hairbrush. She hears them drop, one by one, and roll away beneath her. She is thirsty. She drinks straight from the kitchen tap and feels it fast and cold inside her.

There is a pale reflection of herself in the glass as she

opens the door and steps outside into the garden: an image she recognises as if from a dream. A woman in flux. Visibly changing. Whatever she has been, she leaves behind.

Twigs bend under her as she crosses the grass, trails towards that shadowed space where the cool earth pulses beneath the trees. She waits – the garden waking, singing around her. It comes as only the slightest surprise when she pulls a strand of ivy from her hair and feels a sharp tug at her scalp.

*

Darkness falls and fades, falls and fades – a pattern rippling over her as she grows. She watches the stars turn, milky and scattered. The sense of time passing is so different now.

The house becomes smaller; it is only an oddly shaped, dead thing. The walls are still above her, but she is gaining on them. Months pass. She feels herself creeping into and over the soil, winding her way upwards, expanding slowly into the sky like thunder. When the sun shines again, she swells with nectar. Feet patter over the ground where she is rooted, and winged things shelter in her tangled heart, her pale clusters of flowers, her arms of wood and rope. The soil is rich, she discovers. She takes what she needs, and she gives what she can, and she reaches, stretches for more.

DANCING, NOT FLOATING

JACQUELINE WARD

I

I sat my dolls with their backs against mother's green sofa. My brothers rolled and tumbled across the floor, and Jonny was tuning my dad's radio to Luxemburg. Which was strange because he was a man. I'd understood, until then, that pop music was for kids. Jonny wasn't a kid. He was most definitely an adult with cigarettes and a car.

Last week I'd asked mum if Jonny was an adult.

"Why, Cal? What do you mean, love?"

When I found the words, it felt like someone else was saying them.

"He's not a nice man. Don't talk to strangers."

She laughed. It was loud, with big white teeth and red lipstick.

"He's not a stranger, love. He's daddy's friend. You know him. You know Jonny. I told you before. He needs the money. For a new car."

She flipped through the pages of her magazine.

"But he's..."

Mum had a cross face. I could hear her teeth rubbing against each other.

"I'm sorry if you don't like Jonny, Calista. But mummy needs a break. With daddy." She shook her white hair and blinked a lot. "There's nothing wrong with him. You need to stop this. Now. You're going to secondary school next year."

That day, Jonny sent my brothers upstairs. The radio crackled and finally Tony Prince was telling us he was on a boat. I thought about what mum had said and wondered if secondary school had people like Jonny.

"It's the smallest country in Europe," Jonny said to no one. Because my brothers were chasing each other up and down stairs and I sat with Sindy and Tressy, my dolly friends, on the sofa. We sat very still because no one else was there now. Water whooshed in my ears and my heart thump, thump, thumped. He fiddled with the radio for a while. I could hear my brothers laughing.

I whispered to Sindy, "They'll be back soon." I think he heard me because he turned around and sat on a dining chair.

"Come on, Cally. Come and sit on my knee."

He patted his knee. I looked at Sindy and Tressy. I listened for my dad's car. I knew from last time that if I ran, I could make it upstairs to my room before Jonny caught me. This time he wouldn't catch me.

So, I ran. As fast as I could. Past my brothers. His footsteps quick behind me. I was clutching the girls. Pushing the door and finally inside. We pushed the wicker rocking chair over the doorknob – I thought then that they lent me their strength.

His hand was on the doorknob, and he pushed. Twice. Then he leant against it, and I squeezed my eyes shut, trying my hardest to become invisible. He was gone. I heard his footsteps padding away. He was telling my brothers to go downstairs because he was making them a drink. But I knew that part. I knew it was a trick. I knew he would be back, tiptoeing up the carpet. Into my brother's room to listen at the wall until I thought he had left. But I had the advantage of knowing every creaky floorboard.

I sat the girls on the bed and covered their eyes with their plastic hands. I put a tiny hat on each doll and pulled them over their ears so they wouldn't hear. They didn't need to see this. Or hear it. Even then, as I sat with my back to the door and my feet against my Princess dressing table, I wondered who would cover my eyes and ears.

I I

The sound of a Suzuki 250 was the signal to pull on my leather jacket and zip it up. I'd waited on the stairs, looking left and right for mum and dad to appear. They were in the lounge with their evening gin and tonic, playing at middle-class in a grotesque keeping-up-with-the-Joneses game with the blue-collar neighbours.

I knew all about it. I was doing economics and Mr Wales was all about social class. I saw myself as upwardly mobile, but not in the same way as them. I was driven. I was just about to choose my options for my final two years. I was on the up.

I had a plan. I was going to get out of there, away from them. I was going to university. But first, I was going out with Steve. We would go dancing and then he would drive me around the back of the park. Leader of the Pack. He had his own opinion about them, and he would enlighten me as he sucked on an Embassy number 10.

"Your dad doesn't like me."

That was it, really. Along with various plans to avoid my dad at all costs. It wasn't just my dad who didn't like him. Most of my friends left when he arrived and eyed us suspiciously. I put it down to jealousy back then.

Despite the motor bike oil and the powerful smell of body odour, Steve was very attentive. He made sure that his arm draped over my shoulder and, if I looked away, he would gently turn my chin back towards him.

I used all my wiles to evade my mother's and father's attention. It wasn't difficult because they were looking at each other. The usual suspects tumbled from my lips. My homework, dancing, and friends. I even invented a judo class. I never worked out how they didn't hear the motor bike revving and see me pulling on a crash helmet.

It was a temporary escape, but the crash was still to come. One Monday night, during the under-sixteen disco at the local nightspot, two bouncers escorted Steve outside. I followed him. Big Carl and Al Malone pushed him and called him names I didn't really understand until he walked away. I looked at the bouncers who stood in front of me. I know now that there is always a fork in the road. It's always a decision point. And this was it.

I followed Steve and jumped on the back of the bike. He turned the key in the ignition, and I held on to him as he wheelied past Al and Carl and skidded on the road by the club. He turned and revved and pulled away, and we were speeding toward home. Excitement mingled with fear made me long for my bedroom with Sindy and Tressy and safety.

He turned before the junction and headed away. I shouted for him to stop, but he didn't. Eventually, we arrived outside a house on an estate. He lifted me from the pillion and pulled off my helmet. He looked at the house.

"I live with my granddad. And grandma." He looked down at me. Into my eyes. "You're special. I want you to meet them."

I smiled at him. "But it's nearly ten o'clock. I need to go home."

He laughed. "Are you my girl, or what?"

It all sounded very 1960s. Very Elvis. Doubts kicked, but teenage serotonin surged and cleared the area. Somewhere in the background, I remembered Sandra telling me he was twenty. Or older.

"You have to be to drive a 250. 125's for under seventeens."

Paula Newby telling me Steve was married to someone called Janice. Marriage was eons away. It was something adults do, and I was a child. It came into sharp focus just as he grabbed my hand and pulled me onto the doorstep. He kissed me harder than he ever had and turned his key in the lock.

I saw the glow of the TV under the lounge door and waited for him to turn the handle. Instead, he shouted as he passed.

"Only me. See you in the morning."

Murmurs emerged from the lounge. I tried to turn back. My hand was on the door. Then my feet were missing stairs, and I was falling, then sinking. Deep down. All I could think of was my brothers asleep in their beds and my dolls' hands.

I I I

When I met a proper boyfriend shortly afterwards – which meant someone my age who my parents liked – the whole issue of rolling in at three-thirty in the morning drunk was all but forgotten. By everyone except me. I wasn't drunk. I was terrified.

When Mum opened the door it was almost light.

"Your shirt's buttoned up wrong."

She slapped me. Hard across the face. It left finger-shaped bruises that meant I couldn't go to school for a week. It made it all much worse because I needed normality. They grounded me. Dad pressured me for Steve's address, but I told him I didn't know, which was true. They never asked me what happened. They just assumed the loaded implication that I had done something wrong.

Mum's red mouth crimped in disgust. Dad's disappointment. There was no space between the shame and remorse to tell them. They closed the gaps. It's no wonder I went for Bryn. He was safe. His politeness in front of my parents never quite wore off when we were alone. We dated for five years—throughout sixth form and university. We were inseparable.

He stroked my hair and filled the hole where my happiness should have been. It was an axis of predictability with a few carefully choreographed wild times.

I completed what I needed to, and then I would stare out behind the yellow curtains of our tiny bedsit. Bryn would rub my arm and ask me what was wrong. I learned to smile and stare, to put him off the trail of unsettled torrents I was afraid he would hear.

We graduated together and rented a flat. Mum and dad visited and left satisfied that I had cancelled out my indiscretion. As if a lease and a kettle and toaster set would dam the rapids that tumbled through my thoughts in the middle of the night.

Mum pulled me to one side as Bryn and dad discussed flooring. Her fingers digging into my arm. Her mouth red and smiling but her eyes still scathing.

"So, has he proposed?"

I stared into her Benzodiazepined irises and wondered if this was how you escape. How you hide from the anger and the pining for yourself. Was this the secret every woman learned on their twenty-first birthday? Bryn had dropped marriage hints. He told me I'd better buy a dress because my twenty first was going to be special.

What the day arrived, I climbed into a taffeta number and pinned up my hair. My reflection looked slightly wilder than I expected, but time was short—it would have to do. Bryn instructed me to meet him at the Silver Dollar Restaurant at seven-thirty.

As I walked in, his face changed. Mum and dad looked a little horrified and two of my friends from university smiled widely. Bryn looked surprised. His etched features rarely showed an expression, but he stared at me.

"You look... beautiful."

He even sounded surprised. He was smiling, and I was smiling, but mum's mouth set hard and disapproving. I saw my reflection in my dad's eyes, and I realised what had happened. Cal had reappeared. I had hidden for so long, holding my sadness under, that they had forgotten me. Here I was, in a suburban Chinese restaurant, in all my glory.

The meal went well. Again, carefully planned to the minutest detail so that Bryn could have full control. I felt a strand of hair on my bare shoulder. My dress was a little daring, I conceded, as Sarah Lindop's boyfriend ogled me. Barry pinned the strand back into my curls. It would have been so easy for him to kiss my shoulder, my face. He didn't.

He didn't propose either. In what became a scheduled routine of life according to Bryn, a gaping hole approached between the sixth course of the Special Banquet and the cake. A huddle of servers slightly off-stage waiting for Bryn's signal. My mother's desperation for normality.

They would wait. Bryn calmly skipped to the cake and candles, and only my father's confusion gave it all away. I played my part beautifully, but when we got home, I felt Bryn's discarded jacket for a tiny box I knew would be there. A bump in the smooth road.

He emerged from the bathroom, and I was holding the box. I wanted a scene. I wanted him to tell me he had discovered damaged, shamed me. I wanted him to grab the box and explain. I wanted a reaction. He just looked at me for a long time. Exposed me in my off-the-shoulder gown. Then he spoke.

"You're not a proper woman."

The waves lapped high and threatened to split the surface. Yet I am an expert at holding the dam.

"I am."

He shook his head.

"No. Real women look after their men. Cook. And like it. Clean." He stepped closer. "All you do is fuck and stare."

IV

Michael:

Hey. About last night. I don't want you to think...

Cally:

Yeah. Of course.

Michael:

But you are a nine. Out of ten.

Cally:

Compared with what?

Michael:

Wow, are you some kind of weirdo? Just leave me alone.

V

It was late. I'd just got in. I went out dancing with my friends after work. Life was good on my own and I had a social life. Four of us from work would hit the local nightspot and drink and dance until the early hours. Short black dresses and make-up. But no red lipstick for me. No.

That night I'd laughed until my face was sore. Riding the waves of my singlehood. Before the club we'd been for a curry, and I'd had water to pace myself. It was a work night, and I loved my job in the entertainment section of the city newspaper. I was mid-career, completely devoted to early mornings.

When I closed the door behind me that night and flicked on the lounge-lamp, I felt happy. I kicked off my shoes and flopped onto the sofa, feeling around in my handbag for the change I'd thrown in there after going to the bar.

I don't know what made me see it. The shadow on the slight gap between the curtains. The ever-so-slight movement that caught my attention and super-hyped my senses. I stared into my handbag. A car passed, and I momentarily saw the outline of a person.

I shouted. Not at them. Never at them. I jumped up and opened the kitchen door.

"All right, love. I'll be up in a minute."

I waited. Just the allotted time for a reply played only in my head.

"Yes, yes, OK, I will." I glanced at the window. A sliver of a face through the white curtains. An eye. "I won't be a minute."

I ran to the back door and checked I'd locked it. Then sauntered back into the lounge and casually picked up the phone and dialled 999. I half turned, and the shape was still there, then gone. I ran upstairs and looked up and down the street. It looked deserted. I rushed to the back bedroom and looked into my garden. There were plenty of places to hide.

I sat on the sofa, waiting. Eyes squeezed tightly shut. Hands over ears. Waiting for the police or the shape, whichever came first. The knock on the door startled me, and I stood in the hallway. What if I opened it and it wasn't the police? What if? What if? I went back to the lounge and pulled back the curtain. They'd parked the police car at the end of the road. Two officers were standing looking at my bedroom window.

I let them in. The first one took out a notebook. A tiny black notebook with elastic around it. I almost laughed. It isn't big enough for all I have to say, I thought. I told them what had happened. He wrote it down, then summarised.

"So, you'd been out... dancing? And then you thought you saw a man peering through your curtains?"

I nodded. Not thought. Did. He looked at his colleague.

"Live here on your own, do you?"

I nodded again.

"Right then. If you see anything else, let us know."

I summoned words.

"He probably followed me home."

The second policeman raised his eyebrows.

"From singles night? Isn't it singles night at Donovan's tonight?"

The evidence was building, it seemed. They looked around my lounge and at each other again.

"OK. We'll be off." I guided them to the door and just as he was leaving, the first policeman turned to me. "Here's my number if you ever fancied a drink."

He pushed a card into my hand, and I noted the glint of a thick, gold wedding ring.

VI

I never went to Donovan's again. I made excuse after excuse to not go out with my work colleagues until they stopped asking me. Just before my thirtieth birthday, I sold my lovely house and took a job in Cyprus. It wasn't journalism. I'd bagged a marketing position at a Blue Chip, and I was off to see the world.

They gave me a beautiful apartment and a smart office. It looked out onto the beach, and I spent my days working and swimming. The apartment block had security – I had insisted –and I ventured out at night again.

Two years went by, and I had been seeing a guy from work, Paulo. Just casual for meals out and the occasional lunch. He invited me to a fundraiser where I would meet his friends, and I agreed. I chose my dress carefully. A black number with a slight plunge at the neckline – but nothing trashy. I would wear a wrap to cover my arms.

I'd pulled my hair down and brushed it through. It was long and sun bleached, and I glimpsed my 21st birthday party and almost changed into jeans. The distant taxi horn decided for me. I grabbed my keys and purse and hurried outside. I got into the back.

"Theo's, please."

The taxi driver smiled at me through the mirror.

"Ah. Going with friends?"

I nodded.

"Yes. I'm meeting people. Such a lovely place."

He nodded too.

"It is. Are you regular there?"

"No. Only my second time. I went once when I first came to work here two years ago."

He laughed. I focused on the streetlights and what I would say to Paulo's friends. I pulled the dress hemline down a little, and the neckline up. Maybe I should have chosen better?

I barely noticed when the driver made a right turn towards the mountains. I saw his eyes in the mirror and my reflection in the car window.

"Of course, my husband will be there. He goes there all the time."

He carried on, ever upwards. Losing the streetlights and into the darkness. Then he spoke.

"Children?"

I licked my parched lips and understood the need for lipstick. I was drowning. Drowning. But I trod water.

"A boy and a girl..." I pleaded. I scanned my childless memory and stabbed in the dark. "Lucy and Peter."

He drove on. Then he spoke again.

"Your husband. UK?"

I laughed a little too loudly and covered my left hand. I remembered Maria in my office being married to Spiros. He was a policeman.

"Yes. We come from London. We came here because my husband is working with Spiros Constantineau. He paid for our apartment. He will be there with his wife tonight."

He took the next turn. Across a half-built road and towards the ring road. Bump turned to glide as we hit the smooth tarmac. He stared at me through the mirror.

"Diversion."

I nodded. He dropped me outside Theo's, and I caught the next bus home, staring silently through the window as the bus passed the party.

VI I

Two years later, I was back in London and married. The safety of a second person gravitated me toward the first available person in a rapidly narrowing field.

It happened quickly with John. Six months of dating followed by renting a flat, and then a registry office wedding that neither set of parents attended. It had been a whirl of champagne and white roses. I even had a white dress with a beautiful lacy skirt. But I couldn't wait to get home and feel another person in the same room as me as I slept. The comfort of it persuaded me that all was well. We had even talked about children and, for a fleeting second, I thought that my imaginary Lucy and Peter might materialise.

Jack and I fell into a pattern of me cooking and him sitting on the sofa laughing loudly at Jeremy Clarkson and re-runs of classic comedy. There were arguments, mostly about me being too quiet, but everyone argues, don't they? We had our moments, and under the choppy surface, it all looked like we were madly in love. Yet I knew. He never looked at me. I would hand him a mug of tea and his eyes would not leave the screen.

I would serve dinner and his eyes were on the plate. We went to bed at different times, and he was up before me. Mum had seen it, too. She had blinked at me, the red lipstick bleeding into the lines around her mouth.

"Don't blow it this time, Cally. Marriage is about give and take." Her eyes never left dad as she continued. "Oh. And all the phone calls. Can you just ring once a week? I need a break. With your dad."

My eyes were on Jack. I'd noticed the glances at other women over his shoulder. The unidentified credit card payments late at night. The entirely plausible excuses that he trotted out like learned lines. In the end, it was so obvious. We were watching an episode of The Darling Buds of May, of all things. Jack was a huge David Jason fan and watched him over and over. It required me to laugh at the episodes I knew by heart.

He was laughing extra loud that day. Bellowing and shaking. His eyes never left the screen.

"My god. I never saw it before. You look just like her."

I scanned the screen for a morsel of validation. It was a family scene. They were all there. I felt a pleasure hit as I saw Mariette. Beautiful. Like me, I dared to think. Had he seen me? Had he? He was laughing still.

"You've got a definite look of her. And the pinny."

More laughter. Mariette wasn't wearing a pinny. The only person wearing a pinny was Ma. I pulled in my lips and bit back the tears. This told me everything I needed to know about me, Jack, and my marriage.

VI I I

Dad: Oh hello, love. Your mum's gone to church.

Me: Church? OK.

Dad: OK.

Sound of water running in the background. I picture him in the garden of my childhood home with his back to the house.

Me: So, I just wanted to tell you... me and Jack are getting a divorce.

Silence.

Me: Dad?

Dad: What have you done? What's happened now?

IX

I never learned to drive. I never had the focus or the time. Which is why I found myself on a bus after visiting the undertaker to view mum's body. She wasn't there, it was just flesh with red lipstick and rouge. I couldn't feel her. My brother met me outside.

"The pharmaceutical industry will be in crisis."

He smiled, but I didn't. I got it. I knew she was trying to escape the pain. Escape the feelings. She never got that break with dad. There was always something else she needed to judge or snipe at. Another denial of reality.

I touched her, and she was cold. Dad had brought in a dress for her, and they had done her white hair in a style which made her look different. I never saw her. Not really. She hid herself under self-medication and an armour of piety. As we left, I felt the pull of familiarity and the push of escape. Maybe things would be different now? Was I finally free of the need to behave? No need to dumb myself down.

Time would tell, I thought. But I tested my theory before long. I boarded the bus and paid my fare. I chose a window seat so I could stare out. The rain distracted me, and that is why I didn't notice the drunken couple behind me. I would have sat somewhere else if I had spotted their conspiracy. But as soon as the bus moved, they were giggling.

I felt a pull on my long hair. A single hair popping from my scalp. Giggles turning to laughter. Then silence. I flicked my hair to show them I had felt it. More silence. Then a pull and a click.

The bus was almost full. Someone must have seen it, but no one said a word. Earphones in, staring at phones. No one saw them cut a handful of my hair. No one heard the roaring laughter and the stage whispering.

"I can't believe you did that, mate."

My head told me to stop the bus. Alert the driver. Get the police. I wanted to feel my hair and find out the damage done but years of fear told me not to. They might have scissors. It would draw attention to me and nothing good could come of that.

I sat there. Past my stop. The couple got off just before the terminus, still pointing and laughing helplessly. When I was the only person left on the bus, I lifted my hand to the back of my head and felt the inch-long lengths. I picked up the hair from the floor and put it into my bag.

I went home and told anyone who asked that I had called the police and there had been a big scene.

X

My pixie cut was popular. Three months later I met Alex. He did not care that my hair was short. He was interested in my stare. He made it clear from the start that he walked his own path, and he would be more than happy if I would join him sometimes.

I understood that this was her break; this was what mum told me she wanted all those years ago. She was waiting for a gap in the routine of everyday to ambush dad, peek into his world. Alex was inviting me in. I accepted and eventually invited him to walk with me.

He was consistently kind. And gentle. One evening, high on a hill above my home town, he asked me.

"What happened?" He saw my stare intensify and qualified it quickly. "You don't have to tell me if you don't want to."

I didn't tell him the full story, but he knew. I finally broke the surface tension and asked him a question.

"What is it about me?"

I'd studied myself in the mirror so many times, wondering why. Why all this had happened. He thought for a while then answered.

"You know, people close to us look at us and see the parts we can't see ourselves." He smiled. "I barely know you, but you are a dancer. Glittery shiny and spinning in the cracks between the grey suit and laptop. You should let her out."

A dancer. I nodded and stared out at the lights of the town. He had seen me. Finally, someone had seen me. I flashed back to Bryn and his proclamation.

"I did once."

But look what happened, I wanted to say. Look what happened. I was there, ready to sing and tap dance in my sequins. For all I was worth. But they all wanted someone else. Someone different. Someone who would stay silently in the background, bailing out the water no matter what they did. Not a dancer.

Waves of panic lapped. Dancer. It sounded bad but looked like fun.

"Is that bad? A dancer?"

He smiled. I smiled. High kicks in my heart.

"No. No, it isn't."

And right there, I was dancing and not just floating.

THE PEOPLE'S HISTORY MUSEUM IS CLOSED

HELEN KENNEDY

Manchester is mean and grey. The city sits between the shoulders of the Pennine Moors, cindered from the ashes of sandstone and industry. It's where our childhood burned down. In 1972, you were taken somewhere else for a better life.

"Let's meet at the People's History Museum," you said. It's a place that celebrates democracy and human rights, but I've found that history can be built on unreliable fragments of the past. In some ways, we were never children, it just happened to us. Our childhood is a museum I don't want to visit.

You were born in the middle of the riots. Moss Side burned amber and orange, cars set alight and milk bottles bombs thrown at the police station. The smell of violence. A community sometimes turns on itself when it's hurting. Afterwards, your father disappeared and Carol, the woman who called herself our mother gave up on us. Well, gave up on you – she gave you away.

All journeys to you begin somewhere else.

"The train approaching platform one does not stop here."

I'm going to make the journey to meet you in three legs; Leicester – Sheffield – Manchester. We made our journeys a lifetime ago and I've had fifty years to try and work out the truth of our separation. My husband said, "for God's sake don't drag it all up." But he doesn't know all the people I have been. The things that I regret. I've made my life in Middle England comfort. It was easier to hide amongst the unfamiliar.

It's an expectant morning in Market Harborough, the sun sits above the ridge of Kettering Road. A mother and daughter are arguing in the car park.

"For fuck's sake you must have left it on the kitchen table," the mother says and slams the car door. The girl shrugs.

"This train is formed of seven coaches; first class accommodation is at the front of the train."

Class is a way in which we divide, a way in which we were unbelieved. Poor kids didn't have rights when we grew up.

The train track crackles with electricity. Families have a funny electricity that runs through them but ours was dangerously live. Social workers didn't want to get too near.

I step on board the EMR train and sit facing away from the sun. The view of a neat cricket pitch, lines of houses with back gardens. The fields are divided by flowering hawthorn, green trees in full leaf. Cows sit in a fairy circle, the Welland valley scattered with sheep and lambs.

The young man opposite has two cans of Brewdog lager on the table and he twitches his leg to the ear bud beat. A woman in a hijab rests her head on the table and sleeps. Scoured tracks, allotments and warehouses. A builders yard with bags of gravel. We see life back to front, life from the railway line. Perhaps mine and yours was always the wrong way round? The sun strains to break through the pale light of early morning and I watch my breath fog the window.

"This train will shortly be arriving at Leicester. Please take care when alighting off this train."

The train rattles and shakes as it approaches the station and the guy pings open another can of lager. Its only 8.30am and we all do things to forget. I only come into the city for mammograms and the occasional curry. I don't feel I belong here, and the truth is I don't belong anywhere. That was taken away from us.

In the Pumpkin café, a woman sits on a high stool playing the slot machine, £1 coins lined up in front of her. A plate of gelatinous bacon and sausage sandwiches sits on the counter. Outside tower cranes glide across the sky. A siren wails, an ambulance around the ring road on its way to The Royal *Infirmary.*

"This train is delayed by 34 minutes," the announcement says and the girl in the cropped top and scissor nails pulls a face at her phone. Acid yellow flowers sit in the gravel between tracks: sometimes beauty is found in unexpected things. "Family just got closer with faster trains," the EMR poster says. But our brother-sister bonds were broken when I was chosen and you were given away.

I can remember your cart wheels on the path, the sound of the street. Cars and motorbikes, the threat of noise. Your hair was never cut so it was tight corkscrews and grew as big as a chrysanthemum. Carol didn't bother with things like that, or the truth. She told you your father was dead. His name was Malcolm, but they called him Jeronimo, and after the riots he moved to Neasden. You've probably traced him by now. He wasn't complicit. He didn't look back.

On the day of your accident, I didn't hear the screech of brakes. Swap Shop turned up too loud on the TV drowned out the sound of your thumping head. Carol screamed from the upstairs window, but it was the neighbours who carried you to the ambulance, like a floppy doll. They wouldn't let me come with you and the neighbour Mrs Mackie brought me on the bus.

In the first few days they weren't sure that you would survive, lying in a coma with nurses in white paper crowns coming and going. Your brain rattled in the shell of your skull; your hearing lost to the Manchester ring road.

We came to visit you in hospital, when Carol roused herself from intermittent sleep, and I like to think she felt something. You pointed at your ears, and it took weeks for them to realise that your world was soundless. Your hearing lost. I watched your cheeks fill out with hospital meals of macaroni cheese and chocolate mousse. The nurses spooned love into your mouth. You wore new pyjamas and smiled at everyone.

You didn't come home. The adoption had been planned before the accident, before your world went silent. I never forgave her for it. She didn't care for anything except the dealers at the front door and comatose men in her bed. We weren't a priority.

"Welcome to passengers who have joined us at Leicester. This train will call at Derby, Chesterfield and Sheffield. EMR would like to apologise for the delay in this service."

I wonder if anyone ever apologised to you.

The Belgrave suburbs shine in the sunshine, rows of terraced houses pressed together. This side of the city is known as the Golden Mile. The shop fronts glitter with saris, jewels and red spices. The train picks up speed. The sky grows from the horizon beyond Long Eaton. "Don't get your hopes up," my husband said. What does he know about shaving off pieces of your heart? What can't be cut away is already dead.

The luggage rack is full, but people load on more. The train groans. A girl in Lycra does arm stretches and lads in Nottingham Forest shirts swear like proper fuckers and I'd like to say, "Shut up," but it's not worth the lip they'd give. I've given up saying stuff that doesn't make a difference.

I needed to find you. I filled in forms and made phone calls. The woman at the records office in Wigston High Street put her hand on top of mine as she handed me the file. Sean Thomas Doyle. Adopted 6 August 1972. DOB 07 July 1967. The name and address written in red pen.

After you disappeared things got worse. When the Social came round, Carol swept the gear under the sofa cushions and offered mugs of tea. The house was a tip with sticky carpets, empty bottles and cans. She tidied up the men stripped to the waist, the cuckoo boyfriends she kept. "You'll be best with your mum sweetie," the Social Worker said. They gave me a shiny plastic barbie doll with clean skin and blonde hair that Carol said looked just like me.

Canal boats are tied up along the river Trent. The train guard checks my ticket and scribbles on it. He's wearing a purple waistcoat and I wonder what you will look like. Your wild hair dreads and eyes that used to flicker like gems.

When we came to the hospital to visit, you'd already been taken by the social worker. Carol wasn't sure where. She didn't fight for you. I came home and sat on the bed we shared, Action Man still undressed and your smell on the pillow. You went to a foster family on the other side of the city in garden land, a solid brick semi with a garden path and a shed. It was years before I found out that they just fostered you for a while before you found your real home.

I wasn't adopted. I wasn't chosen. I was abandoned. I left home at fourteen and slept on other people's sofas and in shop doorways for a while. Made money selling Avon and sex. I changed my name to Skye and, for a while, lived in a house with a man called Maz. He had an off licence and I worked behind the counter day and night, but I got wise to that. It didn't last.

Derby is a city of industry. Factories for Rolls Royce engines and train engineering companies push up against the railway lines. A crowd of rowdy students get off the train. The traffic on the ring road is stationary and the air is thick with the smell of it.

The train jolts as it starts to move and I spill my coffee, almost instinctive. It stains my best dress muddy brown and I rub at it with my hand.. Derbyshire breaks out into hills. The folds of fields and the shell of hillsides purpled with heather and scrub. Stone wall breaks. The young man sitting beside me with a tight top knot, stretches and yawns. Walkers in waterproofs pack and repack their rucksacks, producing cakes wrapped in cling film from their pockets. Long lines of wires and telegraph poles relay communications across the dales. The wide river moves lazily along as the train sways and rolls through the landscape. Steep embankments and cows on a hillside. It's strangely comforting.

After you left, Carol overdosed. She was brought back to life and had a spell in hospital but by then she'd been chucked out of the house. When I went round all her clothes were thrown in the front garden. I sorted through our things, old toys and blankets. Your Action Man jeep left to rot with the white goods and the sofa. The neighbours offered me tea and a chat, but I didn't want to hang around. It was a long time before I ever felt safe.

I think Jeannie and Des, your adoptive parents, loved you. They had your graduation photo on the telly, a boy in a cap and gown and yellow sash. Engineering, first class honours. They invited me in and talked nonstop about you, everything from mini rugby to playing the drums. Jeannie showed me your old room with the Manchester United bedspread and posters on the walls. Almost a shrine. I asked them for your phone number and a look passed between them. Des put his hand on my arm and said, ok but they'd have to ask you first. That they'd be in touch. I didn't hear from you for over a month and thought that opening up the past must have been too painful for you.

Housing estates around Chesterfield are flat and white. It's a town of roundabouts, and a church with a wonky spire like an ice cream cone sits above the hillside. A party of hen girls in bunny ears and heels get on the train and crush into seats together, fleshy and energised. Two men kiss on the platform and one of them jumps into the carriage just before it moves off. The train has made up time and I wonder if I can. We pick up speed.

I don't know where you went next; parts of your life aren't filled in and neither is mine. There's a lot in silence. I slept with men old enough to be my father, although I didn't know him. I felt unwhole, unwholesome. Split in two. I was your voice, and I yet didn't have one of my own. But the truth is that you were fine without me.

Dawn, the key worker with the red hair tried to find me a bed in a hostel. I moved into one just behind Oldham Street with red curtains at the window, slept behind the door because it felt unsafe. The Social gave me a photograph of you, sat on a wall outside Hulme Road adoption centre, your smile from ear to ear and perfect white teeth. A photograph can speak, and I can hear your new family saying, "he's such a nice kid," off camera. I keep that photograph in my purse; its kept me safe over the years.

I heard that Carol had died through a newspaper cutting in the Manchester Evening News. It highlighted the problem of long-term addiction in Manchester. The journalist had tried to contact me, apparently to talk about drugs counselling. I didn't go to Carol's funeral, but afterwards I sometimes wished I had. Perhaps I could have left my anger buried with her. I think we were her only family, you and me. She never talked about anyone else, I wasn't even sure where she had been born. We were all rootless.

South Yorkshire feels like freedom, something of its wilderness and room to breathe.

"All change for Sheffield please. All change."

Sheffield sits between the sky and the granite of South Yorkshire. New high-rise apartments and steel city offices. Northern Trains are unreliable, unconnected. Three services from Newcastle to Liverpool are cancelled, and the platform is heaving with people and luggage. The heat from the tracks chokes. A mother with three kids abandons their suitcases and goes off to get drinks. "Mind them for me love," she calls over her shoulder. I realise that my hands are shaking.

The psychologist says that everything we do in life is connected to the past. I wasn't ever sure that I could go forwards, tied down with guilt. I didn't know my father, and when I asked Carol about him, she shrugged and said my guess was as good as anybody's. I have a memory of lighting a cigarette for her whilst her lips quivered. The match burned my fingers and I realised that she didn't care. I ran my hand under the kitchen tap and let the water soothe it, but the tips of my fingers were white, scorched. Sometimes Carol couldn't rouse herself from sleep and the dreamy days were sat in the garden playing with Barbie in the long grass. Sometimes neighbours brought round a packet of Jammie Dodgers and a drink of pop.

The mother at the station reappears with armfuls of sandwiches and packets of crisps. The three children sit on their luggage and tear open packets. I smile as I watch them and realise that I am staring. "Always hungry," the woman says.

I find a seat in the last carriage. The train creaks and groans out of Sheffield for its journey across the Pennine Moors, the backbone of the country. I know now that you moved to Wakefield, got a first job in design engineering, a new girlfriend and a car. You made a good start to life. The Northern trains announcements are so quiet I can't hear them. I wonder what you hear, what you choose to hear.

"Remember what you have here with us," my husband said and I think about the small house on Windermere Drive, my two grown up children and a job at the Co-op. The second half of my life has been almost textbook.

A man from the Salvation Army helped get me my first flat, a one bedder in the city centre, a table and chair and a Baby Belling. I went to Salford Tech and trained in hairdressing and beauty therapy, worked in a nail bar in the Arndale centre. It paid the bills. Gradually, I saved a few quid here and there, bought a car and went mobile, doing perms and sets for women who couldn't get out and about. I loved that work, cups of tea and chats, regular money from people who knew my name. Women who relied on me.

I was scared to be a mother; it felt too much of a responsibility. I breathe long and slow through my hands. I do that when my HRT isn't working. The heat under my skin feels tight and yet I know it's you who has the right to feel angry. I found you living in San Sebastian. Your partner, Carlos is a wine merchant, a man in his sixties. It's a different light in San Sebastián, open to possibilities. You paint seascapes; blue and violet shapes of the sea. New places to escape to. I've seen your art for sale on the internet. Distance opens up a new perspective on the world.

The scars of the Yorkshire landscape soon become clear. Rocky outcrops and moorland. The wind moves the tall trees. Open fells and fields where lambs lie in the crook of stone walls. The Northern train rumbles and leans into the hillside. White caravans stand in rows in the dip of the valley at Bamford. And you'd need to be a goat to climb the sides of the fell at Grindleford. A path snakes to the top of the hill and I think about rolling, about tumbling down the bank at the Clough. Outdoors was our chance to escape, to feel the cool grass in our faces. Long summer days when we were carefree. But there was always the end of the day, the sun going down and the thought of going home.

I've suddenly feel hollow and realise I've not eaten. I reach in my handbag and find a packet of Polo's. My husband says that I'm a good person, that I can't carry on being the villain. Sometimes the anger sits just beneath my breastbone and is hard to shift. Therapy has helped and sometimes emptied everything on the floor. It's taken years to unbury the past, moments when I didn't want to go on.

The train slips into another tunnel, moving from one county to another in darkness. Who gets to decide if one life is better than another? The carriage scrapes on the tracks, metal on metal. The shudder of brakes. The momentum slows and I think, God no, not now. Don't break down.

I didn't expect that you would agree to come to meet me. Why would you? Your life on the waterfront, with seafood and wine. I stalked you on Facebook for a while, watching your life spin in a faster orbit. Dinners and art exhibitions, holidays around the Med, always Carlos by your side. Who needs the past? But you wrote back and said, "Michaela, I need to do this."

There were moments when it could have been different. I could have begged the social worker for a new place for us both. Somewhere we could be together. But no one wanted a deaf mixed-race boy and a girl with bad teeth who looked half her age.

The train slides into the echo of an embankment, silence as we skim underground. The carriage plunged into darkness. We emerge to a new pattern of fields and stone walls, a stone byre set in the shell of the hillside. Heather in purple and black, peppered with sunlight. Lancashire has a solidness to it. A sky that sits proudly above the landscape with high clouds that scurry eastwards. The day breaks into splintered sunshine and I feel hopeful. People in the carriage get restless, checking their phones and pulling down bags from the overhead shelf. The man beside me pulls out the buds from his ears and shakes himself awake. A small excitement ripples the train.

I feel suddenly nervous. Years of searching databases and phone books, trawling the internet for traces of you. My husband texts me a smiley face and a message, "Be brave." He's a kind man who has learned about my past in outbursts. He doesn't ask too many questions and when the words won't come, he holds me until I feel safe. We married late, but love can be uncompromising in its intensity. We were both making up for lost time, partners and lives we left behind. Love is a place where we don't have to be better than we really are.

The countryside gives way to concrete and industry. I see Manchester from a distance, sheltered inside the bowl of the West Pennines, the city grounded in the landscape. High rise steel shuttered buildings, the shine of Spinningfields. The skyline is busy with swinging tower cranes, the thump of construction. New apartments are being built everywhere. It feels alive. You smell the city before you arrive; the takeaways and the bus lane diesel. Urbanity stretched to its limits with warehouses and factories, tethered by the rise and fall of the Mancunian Way. The bird's nest of the Etihad stadium sits on the skyline.

The train pulls into Piccadilly station and groans to a halt. I've been here a thousand times and it still makes my heart stop. Fourteen platforms under glass, the air hot and acrid. Trains grind their way here from all across the country. Manchester is proud, magnificent in the sunshine. But it's polarising. I've not been back here for years.

"You can do this Mum," my son Rory said. But I haven't told him that I was responsible, that it was all my fault. My son isn't like me. He is brave and honest, and still dreams. There are things about me that he says are quirky, my hesitancy to be photographed, my endless cleaning and love of dancing. My sobriety. Being a mum has kept me focussed on someone else. Rory never fails to make me laugh; he is his father's son.

Over the years, I've come to forgive Carol, to feel sorry for her. We never knew her parents, and she had called so many people Mum. In and out of care, but never cared for. She was an inadequate mother but I've made sure that she has never defined me. I am my own person.

I walk across Piccadilly Gardens where the tram tracks draw steel parallel lines. The hum of electric is oddly comforting. "We are not a Petri dish," is graffitied on a concrete wall. Rough sleepers lie on benches in the sunshine. The shop windows of Primark and the closed down shell of Debenhams reflect the light across the square. I have a distinct memory of Selnec buses dip dyed in orange and yellow circling this city. Sitting on the front seat of the top deck with you by my side. Excited for a trip to the shops and a comic from WH Smith's. The truth is this is our city, it's where we were born. Sometimes we can't distance ourselves from the people we were and the places we came from. Sometimes we can't leave them behind.

The People's History Museum is closed. It sits on the Left Bank, overlooking the river Irwell. Deep and dark and unmagical. The high building set in honey-coloured stone, a triumph of a city examining its past, planning its future. I sit on the outside terrace and stare at the fragments of blue sky, close my eyes. Childhood is a museum I don't want to visit. But we have the present and a future.

I see you before you see me. You're wearing shorts and a linen shirt, sunglasses pushed on the top of your head. Your hair cut short and grey, still wiry. A familiar smile ear to ear. You look younger than I expected, relaxed. I hesitate. There are moments in life that are fixed in time. I have waited for this one for a long time.

You reach out to hug me; it feels instinctive. You stand taller than me, broad shouldered. The smell of expensive cologne. We hold on to each other, neither wanting to break off.

"You came," I whisper. There is a small hearing aid lodged behind your left ear, and you place your finger on it.

"A new implant," you say. "I'm like the bionic man."

Your life in all its spectacular noise; its my life that has been soundless. You take a step back to look at me and I feel disappointing. A middle-aged woman with her life's baggage.

I take a deep breath.

"It was my fault," I say. The words won't come quick enough. "I told Carol that we'd be better off without you, that it would be easier just her and me." You don't look at me. "It was all my fault that you were taken away."

We stand for a moment, our childhoods between us. Your eyes still shine like gems. "It's ok," you say. "I think I had the better time of it to be honest." You smile again and lean in to kiss my cheek and I feel the weight of everything.

"How was your journey?" you say. The world spins but time doesn't change who we are. Across cities and suburbs, fields and moorland. We are carved like the landscape.

"Too long," I say. We watch the river Irwell flow, making its journey to the open sea.

Author Biographies

Helen Kennedy holds an MA (Distinction) in Creative Writing from Oxford Brookes and a diploma from the University of Oxford. Her short stories have been published and shortlisted by The Bristol Prize (2022), The Oxford Flash Fiction Prize (2023), TSS Cambridge Prize, Faversham Lit Prize (2022), Reflex, Flash 500, Retreat West, Story Nook, and National Flash Fiction Day (2022) as part of their new writers series.

She has recently completed a short story collection, 'Acts of Identity Vandalism,' a novella, 'Missing Pieces,' about the disappearance of a girl in a northern town, and is completing a debut novel, 'Blessed Women,' a love letter to strong Salford women.

Katie Hale is the author of a novel, My Name is Monster, and two poetry pamphlets. She is a former MacDowell Fellow, and winner of the Palette Poetry Prize, Munster Chapbook Prize, and Prole Laureate Competition. Her short fiction has been longlisted for the BBC National Short Story Award. Katie also runs Dove Cottage Young Poets for Wordsworth Grasmere, and is a Core Team Member of the Writing Squad. In 2022, she won the Northern Writers' Award for Fiction for her second novel – and her debut poetry collection, White Ghosts, comes out with Nine Arches in March 2023.

Louise Finnigan is a short story-writer and novelist from Manchester. She has been shortlisted for the Manchester Fiction Prize, the Cambridge story prize and the Bristol prize. Her story Muscle and Mouth made its debut with Fly on The Wall Press as part of their 2021 shorts series.

Jacqueline Ward is a writer from the Oldham. She is a psychologist and her debut novel, PERFECT TEN, was published by Corvus Atlantic Books in 2018. Her second novel, HOW TO PLAY DEAD, was published in November 2019. Her next novels, TEENAGE KICKS, a comedy tragedy set in Manchester's Northern Quarter, and domestic noir THE REPLACEMENT are published early 2023 with two further titles in 2024.

Acknowledgements and Thanks

Helen Kennedy: Thank you to Isabelle Kenyon and FOTW for finding a home for my words and giving opportunities to new writers. A big shout out to all my lovely writer friends (you know who you are!) who have supported me- and to Gaynor Jones and Sally Bayley for words of wisdom. A special thanks to my amazing daughter, Scar Kennedy who has made me brave.

About Fly on the Wall Press

A publisher with a conscience.
Political, Sustainable, Ethical.
Publishing politically-engaged, international fiction, poetry and cross-genre anthologies on pressing issues. Founded in 2018 by founding editor, Isabelle Kenyon.

Some other publications:

The Sound of the Earth Singing to Herself by Ricky Ray

We Saw It All Happen by Julian Bishop

Odd as F*ck by Anne Walsh Donnelly

Imperfect Beginnings by Viv Fogel

These Mothers of Gods by Rachel Bower

Sin Is Due To Open In A Room Above Kitty's by Morag Anderson

Fauna by David Hartley

How To Bring Him Back by Clare HM

Hassan's Zoo and A Village in Winter by Ruth Brandt

No One Has Any Intention of Building A Wall by Ruth Brandt

Snapshots of the Apocalypse by Katy Wimhurst

Demos Rising

Exposition Ladies by Helen Bowie

A Dedication to Drowning by Maeve McKenna

The House with Two Letterboxes by Janet H Swinney

Climacteric by Jo Bratten

Cracked Asphalt by Sree Sen

Social Media:

@fly_press (Twitter) @flyonthewallpress (Instagram)

@flyonthewallpress (Facebook)

www.flyonthewallpress.co.uk